THE TAYLOR STREET FILE OF
LEG MEN

JoBe Cerny

Cerny / American Creative
CHICAGO

CERNY/AMERICAN CREATIVE, LLC
www.actorsaudio.com

This is a work of fiction. Names, characters, places, events, and incidents are either the product of the author's imagination or are used fictitiously. The author's use of places or businesses is not intended to change the entirely fictional character of the work. In all other respects, any resemblance to persons living or dead, businesses, companies, events, or locales is entirely coincidental.

ISBN: 978-0-9916685-1-9
Library of Congress Control Number: 2017932767

Printed in the United States of America
First Edition

THE TAYLOR STREET FILE OF
LEG MEN

BACKGROUND

AT MIDNIGHT ON MARCH thirtieth of 1931, Tug Collier, a Chicago undercover police detective, was shot in the back. A few minutes later, an unidentified blonde woman who was in his car, was shot between the eyes. On her person was a large sum of cash. Three fellow undercover officers cleaned up the mess and kept the murders a secret because Tug Collier was an American spy and assassin who had survived countless missions during World War I. To this day, his war records are regarded as classified information.

He returned home after the war and became a Chicago undercover detective during Prohibition. Little is known about most of his police work because all of his case files are classified—just like his military files.

On the night he was murdered, the undercover unit that went to his house on Taylor Street made an amazing discovery: Detective Collier was a wealthy man. Since he had no family, he left his entire estate to a trust that the police department euphemistically refers to as "The Widows' and Orphans' Fund." The trust's directors made wise investments and grew the fund into a self-sustaining eternal trust to help cops who are down on their luck. Tug Collier even set aside money so his Taylor Street house could be used as a home for ex-cops who need help getting back on their feet.

Paperwork is the bane of detectives, and Tug Collier's classified files were eventually forgotten. The police department has no knowledge of their whereabouts and it is assumed they have all been lost or destroyed. These days, Tug Collier's Taylor Street house no longer exists, although it is still there in spirit. The detectives who know about it refer to it as "Taylor Street." These days, the Widows' and Orphans' Fund also supports a private detective agency of suspended police detectives.

My name is Frankie Turk. I am an ex-cop with an honest streak. I went a little too far pursuing justice and got suspended from the Chicago Police Department. So, until I'm reinstated, I'm working private cases out of Taylor Street. I "unofficially" help the Chicago Police do things they are not supposed to do. What follows is The Taylor Street File of ... **LEG MEN.**

HORSING AROUND WITH MY DAD

I WAS FIVE YEARS OLD when my dad took me to my first Fourth of July parade in Chicago. He told me it was going to be something very special that I'd remember for the rest of my life. I was so young I don't remember a lot, but what I do remember has stuck with me.

There were huge crowds of people. I was short; so at first, all I saw was legs. I felt like I was lost in a forest of legs. The parade wasn't much fun until my father lifted me up onto his shoulders. Then I could see what everybody else saw.

There were bagpipers in kilts marching down the street in columns, their hairy legs moving in unison. There was music. There were lots of flags. What I remember most vividly was seeing a policeman in a blue uniform sitting on a white horse. The horse was very beautiful. It looked like it wanted to run, but the policeman kept it under control.

He stopped the horse next to us. I asked my dad who the man was. He told me the man was a policeman and he was there to protect people. I asked him why the policeman was on a horse. He said because the horse was very fast and could outrun any man. I liked the policeman's dark-blue uniform with the brass buttons. He had a gun like my toy six-shooter, which was my favorite toy.

But I liked the horse even more. I asked my dad if I could pet the horse. My dad edged me closer to the horse and asked the policeman if I could pet it. The policeman said yes and told me to pet the horse's nose because his horse liked that. I reached out and stroked the horse's nose. It was very soft. The horse's breath was warm, and when he snorted it made me laugh. As they walked away, the policeman waved good-bye and the horse looked back at me and bobbed its head as if to say, "See you later, partner." That was the moment I decided to be a policeman when I grew up.

WHAT ARE THE ODDS?

FOR SOME REASON, NOT too many Chicago cops ride horses anymore. I guess it cuts down on the number of bow-legged cops. Whenever I do see a policeman on horseback, it reminds me of that Fourth of July parade when I decided to pursue a career in law enforcement.

My ex-wife, Lola Lahti, and I are cops. We were both suspended for bending the rules. We share a common belief that rules and paperwork should never take precedence over common sense when it comes to enforcing the law and protecting the public. Good police officers and detectives are like good soldiers: they do what they have to do and then sort the paperwork out later.

These days, bad guys get away with murder—and that isn't right. It was a lucky thing that Lola and I were suspended at the same time because we were assigned to the Taylor Street unit at the same time, and that brought us back together.

9

Our continuing relationship remains a work in progress. As of now, we are officially private investigators who unofficially help the police. Quite frankly, being suspended freed us up to pursue justice in a less-structured environment. Our new jobs are more fulfilling, and the pay is much better.

As far as we're concerned, our suspensions were more of a promotion. The only drawback is our current living accommodations. Since we work undercover, we're always in limbo. Taylor Street is not a place as much as it is a number of safe-haven locations, and we are constantly on the move so no one can get a fix on either of us. As a result, whenever we want to, we can move to a safer location and become invisible, which is pretty handy since neither of us is a comic book superhero.

Our latest assignment was just west of the Chicago city limits. That's the part of Chicago where they still have the most horses. Once upon a time, the west side had four racetracks where people could bet the ponies. Is it any wonder that the mob was located on the west side back in the days of Prohibition and the Great Depression?

Two of the old racetracks are long gone. Washington Park burned to the ground and Sportsman's was torn down so an auto speedway could be built there. Unfortunately, the speedway only lasted a few years before it failed financially and was torn down. But the ponies are still running at the grand, old racetracks of Chicagoland. One is located in Al Capone's old stomping ground, Cicero. The other is located farther west of Chicagoland.

The west side is also the home of polo. If you're interested in the sport of polo, Oak Brook is a place where even Prince Charles has played. Polo is kind of like guys playing hockey on horseback. I remember one of my history teachers saying the Mongol Hordes invented polo. But they didn't whack around a little white ball like the guys at Oak Brook—they used the decapitated heads of their enemies. I doubt that would be legal anymore, but if it was, it would probably be the number one rated show on pay-per-view cable. Regardless, the west side is the best side if you want to see horses in Chicago.

"What are the odds?" That basically sums up the business of thoroughbred horse racing. People attend horse races to bet money. A horse racetrack is a business where the odds are controlled by the odds makers at the track. Their job is to set the odds so that the track makes money. In the vast majority of the cases, no matter how much the public bets or how much they win, the house still makes a profit. And the profit is about ten percent, which is a better result than the most conservative bankers achieve. Each person who bets thinks they can beat the odds. But, in the long run, they can't beat the odds. Bettors say horse racing is entertainment, and most of them profess to love the "nobility of the sport of kings." But, how many people would pay to watch horse racing if betting wasn't allowed? Zero. The simple reality is betting is the entertainment—not the races, not the horses, and not the nobility of the sport of kings. Auto racing is exciting, but there are no betting windows at automotive speed-ways. Why? Horse races take two minutes; car races take hours. Why make one bet a day when you can make ten or twelve?

A word of warning: gambling is addictive.

I think it is interesting to compare the intelli-gence of the businessman who runs the track to the gamblers who frequent the track, to the intel-ligence of the horses that race at the track. The businessman operates the track like a business, which takes a lot of intelligence. He does a lot of homework each day to set the odds so that he is guaranteed a ten percent profit. He makes adjust-ments to the odds right up until the moment the betting windows close so that his business is guaranteed to make a profit.

The professional gambler places a bet know-ing the odds are set at a ten percent disadvantage. The average gamblers bets on every race, and one out of every eleven times they spend a day at the races, they come home a big winner—which keeps them coming back. When an average fan loses, he doesn't talk about it.

A horse has less intelligence than a dog. A horse is only smart enough to get all four of its legs to run. The instinct to run is bred into a thoroughbred racehorse, so it might not even need to use its limited intelligence to run—it probably does it instinctively. Instinct tells the horse that if it outruns all of the other horses it will survive. Instinct also tells a horse that if it is the slowest horse, it will be eaten if it falls behind the pack. Once upon a time, wolf packs stalked herds of horses and thinned the herds by killing and eating the slowest and weakest horses. Darwin called it "survival of the fittest." Today, things work out pretty much the same way pretty much the same way—winning horses generate stud fees and live long lives, and the horses that frequently lose are sold for dog food.

I've often thought it would be more interesting if the bettors wagered on the jockeys instead of the horses, but a potential problem with that is jockeys control the horses, and jockeys are human, so they can cheat. Cheating, like losing, is a concept that racehorses don't understand. Horses are honest; people are not. Horses always want to run fast. The very best jockeys want their mounts to run fast. All of the best jockeys make a lot of money. Jockeys get paid a nominal amount to ride each race because the majority of their earnings come from their share of the purse. Each race has a cash prize for the owner, and the jockey gets a share of it. As in any sport, there are winners and losers. There are famous jockeys who are millionaires, but most jockeys risk life and limb and never achieve fame or fortune. Those are the jockeys who make gambling a risky proposition. All jockeys know their survival is dependent upon beating the odds. When a million-to-one-shot comes across the finish line, the crowd screams because an underdog horse triumphed. However, the racing commission, odds makers, track officials, and leg men of the mob investigate "miracles" because they don't believe in them. At a racetrack, hundreds of betting windows make gambling convenient. Only cash wagers are accepted at betting windows. Winning bets are paid out in cash, and no one has to present an ID to place or collect a bet. Could any system be more imperfect? That is why gambling is always risky and potentially dangerous. And that is why Lola and I were excited about our new assignment.

A HOMELESS MAN BEGS TO DIFFER

EARLY IN THE MORNING, Lola and I were notified of our new assignment by text. I felt a vibration in my pocket, and saw **"Post Office Box 824"** come up on my phone's screen. It was a gorgeous July day, so Lola and I decided to walk to the post office. I had been given a heads-up about our next assignment a couple days earlier by our contact in the police department, Captain Danny Doyle. I looked forward to the job because it involved a thoroughbred racehorse. As we approached the entrance to the post office, a legless man in a wheelchair held out a cup to me. I felt sorry for him. Once in awhile I drop change in a beggar's cup, but there is always a beggar in front of the post office, and it's like having to feed a parking meter each time I want to go inside. I didn't have any change, so I decided to avoid him. I find it easier to avoid dropping money in a beggar's cup if I don't look the beggar in the eye.

15

So today, I kept talking to Lola as we passed the legless man. The automatic doors opened as we neared the entrance, and we gained entry to the post office without spending a dime. We walked directly to Box 824 and opened it. Inside was a small package that was mailed from Marguerite Spangler from a post office in Pleasant Ridge, Illinois. Inside the package we found our assignment and a cash down payment for our services. (Taylor Street has been a green company from the very beginning, accepting only cash payments for services; no checks, no credit cards, or payment plans accepted.) We always request payment in big bills because it makes counting the cash faster. While Lola counted the cash, I read the assignment. She smiled when she counted the cash, but I frowned when I read the letter because we were hired to be bodyguards for a thirteen-year-old girl who owned a racehorse. I handed the letter to Lola and she read it, but she continued to smile and said, "Lighten up, Frankie. Maybe we can have a pajama party and help each other paint our toenails."

As we walked out of the post office, the legless man was standing up. When I saw that he had legs, I felt like turning him upside down and shaking the money out of his pockets. As we passed him, he whispered, "Frankie, I see you got your assignment." He held out his hand. "I'm detective Johnny Rice. I work undercover. Your buddy,

Danny, made me your leg man for this case."
He pointed to an old Chevy Astro van that was
illegally parked in front of the post office. "How
about if we take a ride down Ogden Avenue and
get an Italian Beef at Novi's?"

He somehow knew my weak spot when it
came to lunch; so he didn't have to ask twice. I
think positively, and religiously devote an extra
hour at the gym every time I eat one. I always
order a "sweet beef," which is thickly cut pieces
of sweet green peppers simmered in spices and
juices and placed on top of the beef. But, you can
also order a beef sandwich with whole, hot green
peppers or you can get a combination of sweet
and hot peppers. Lola likes her beef with *giardiniera*, which is a mixture of hot peppers and other
mysterious vegetables. (Don't try to figure out
how to pronounce *giardiniera* because everyone
mispronounces it differently, and if the counter
guy sees you're having trouble saying it, he'll
point to it and put it on your sandwich.)

Johnny Rice knew how to make friends
quickly. Although Novi's Beef Stand was built
way before drive-thru windows were vogue, it
had one but almost nobody used it. Most people
wanted to go inside so they could just smell
the place. It was impossible to walk in and out
of Novi's without your mouth watering. They
also serve fries, which can only be described as
crispy perfection. And, in case you're wondering,

everyone who orders a genuine Italian Beef sandwich also orders a jumbo Coca-Cola to wash it
all down. We also got fries, which can only be
described as golden, crispy perfection. Our friend
Nancy Barone owns the place and always waits
on us. Lola went to school with Nancy, but since
it was lunchtime, which was Novi's busiest hour,
none of us had time to catch up. Instead, we got
legs on the Italian Beefs, and Johnny drove us to
a stone quarry in Stickney, just south of the Burl-
ington tracks, to enjoy what we thought would be
a nice little picnic.

CHICAGO'S GRAND CANYON
BECOMES DEATH VALLEY

JOHNNY PARKED THE ASTRO van under the shade of a dusty, old oak tree on the top of the quarry. How it managed to continue to suck enough water out of the stone to survive was an eternal mystery to me. Its longevity had to be some sort of survival lesson.

Johnny took three folding beach chairs out of the van, and we lunched under the shade of the old oak, enjoying the view high above Illinois' miniature version of the Grand Canyon. While that sounds glorious, I don't recommend the dusty quarry as a family vacation destination, but it was a pleasant change of pace for Lola and me. It was quiet, peaceful, and deserted. When you eat an Italian Beef sandwich, you don't talk much. They're both a handful to hold and a very full mouthful to chew. So, first we ate; then we burped and let our stomachs settle, which took about five minutes. I finally broke the silence and asked Johnny, "So, this assignment we picked up is for real?"

Before he answered, Johnny produced old-fashioned, flat, wooden toothpicks so we could gracefully pick the beef out from between our teeth. I always get food stuck under my right molar cap so I carry a floss pick with me every-where, but I wasn't going to use a floss pick in front of a fellow officer. I gratefully accepted the toothpick. Johnny smiled when I took it and I noticed he had a gold front tooth; the other one was regular. His dentist had left a star of enamel in the center of the gold tooth. It was an old-school attention-getter, like a pierced tongue with a diamond stud is today. After we all picked for awhile, he answered my question. "Sure as hell, yes, this assignment is for real! You don't think I brought you out here to just picnic and pick your teeth, did you? I mean, this is just a stone quarry in Stickney—it ain't the Grand Canyon. (Johnny and I were on the same page with that fact.) A little birdie gave me a tip this morning, and I passed it on to someone who should be arriving shortly. In the meantime, how about we take a little walk and work off some of the calories? I got something I want to show you."

A family-owned company had been mining gravel out of the quarry since before Fred Flint-stone made quarries family fare on television. The supply of gravel seemed to be endless. Each year, as they dug lower and lower into the bedrock, they always left a road so they could get equipment up and down and to and from the worksite. One of the neat things about the quarry was there was always a lake somewhere at the bottom of it. The location of the lake constantly changed because as they dug lower, the water flowed to the lowest level and made a new lake. The water always looked crystal clear and inviting. Since I had just eaten a beef sandwich, I knew I'd have to wait at least an hour before I could go swimming. But when we reached rock bottom, I didn't feel like swimming any longer. As I looked out across the shimmering water, I saw a fully clothed jockey in red-white-and-green racing silks floating face down in the water.

EVERYBODY SWEATS, BUT WHO DRINKS MANGO GATORADE?

JOHNNY TOLD US HE got an anonymous tip about the dead jockey. He called the county coroner earlier in the day and told him to bring a body bag and an ambulance and meet us at the quarry after lunch. Since the quarry was in an unincorporated area, no one else except the county coroner was going to respond to the call. Johnny didn't know how the body got in the drink, but we figured it was going to have something to do with our assignment. I'm a pretty good talker, so I decided to stay with Johnny, hoping to get some insights into what was going on. Lola excused herself so she could stretch her very long, shapely legs and take a little nature hike around the lake.

The county coroner's name was McGoonin. I remembered it from his election posters. Traditionally, political campaign posters are printed in red for Republicans and blue for Democrats. But

McGoonin was running for coroner so he printed his campaign posters in orange and black, the colors of Halloween, with a little black hearse on the poster. He ran as an independent for the Halloween Party and won by a landslide. It was nice having a coroner with a sense of humor. He didn't need television commercials, a slogan, a smear campaign, or anything else. He had the perfect name for a coroner and the right choice of graphics. When he arrived on the scene, he waved to us from the top of the quarry, and Johnny motioned for him to drive down to us.

When he reached the bottom, he walked over to us and shook our hands. When I first laid eyes on McGoonin, I instantly knew why he didn't do any television commercials: he was as obese as a sumo wrestler, he sweated like a pro football lineman, and he waddled like a duck when he walked. The sun was high overhead and the temperature at the bottom of the pit was well over a hundred degrees. Johnny pointed to the dead body floating in the water. It was like someone plucked him off of a horse right after a race. The sun had warmed the body, and it was starting to swell and smell. There was no doubt in my mind that this jockey would never make weight again. The coroner's crew wore respirators as they fished the body out of the water. All in all, it was a procedure I never wanted to see again. McGoonin had sweated through his white shirt, and sweat was dripping off his tie in rivulets as he examined the body and made notes. Then his crew put the jockey into a black body bag and zipped it up. McGoonin took off his rubber gloves and shook hands with us. Then the coroner and his crew departed with the body.

"McGoonin sure can sweat," said Johnny. "He is a heart attack just waiting to happen."

"I couldn't agree with you more," I replied. "How did you know the jockey was down here?"

"I told you. I'm your leg man," Johnny answered. "They turn me loose on the street to find things out. I got a tip, and I checked it out. I live my job. I go here and there gathering up odd and interesting pieces of information. When I find a juicy tidbit, I let it be known to my people in the department, and they figure out what to do with it."

"The jockey was beyond juicy."

Johnny laughed and said, "That's for sure."

"Who are your 'people'?"

"If I told you that, I'd have to kill you," Johnny joked.

"Thanks for the update. I'll take you at your word. So, what has this got to do with our baby-sitting job?"

"How about we round up your partner, and I tell you when we get back in the shade of the van. I got a cooler of beer up there."

I spotted Lola on the other side of the pit and called her on my cell phone. Lola must have been surprised when her phone rang because I saw her reach for her gun before she reached for her cell. When she answered, I said, "Lola, want to have a beer with Johnny and me?"

"I can't. I've got a softball game tonight. But, after my experience here in Death Valley this afternoon, I'm going to need to be attached to an IV of Gatorade until game time. Let's get out of here. I feel like I'm being flame-broiled. I'll meet you at the road that we came down. The walk back up it will be a killer." We didn't talk much as we trudged back to the top of the gravel pit. None of us sweated like McGoonin, but who would want to? Johnny had locked his Astro van up tight, so when we finally reached it, the temperature inside was about 130 degrees. He pulled out the cooler, and we gathered around it to feel the cool air rise. It was filled with Gatorade instead of beer. I was disappointed, but Lola was beside herself. "What gives, Johnny?" I asked.

"I told you, I'm a leg man. I know everything about you two. I know Lola has a game tonight. I hear you got a gun for an arm, girl."

"I also got a gun for my hand, and six rifles in my closet for special occasions,"Lola replied.

"I know that, too. I've been in your closet. The force had me keep close tabs on you when you worked your first Taylor Street case. You didn't think they were just going to turn you two loose like mad dogs, did you?"

I responded, "Yeah, I did."

Suddenly, we both felt naked. Johnny knew too much about us.

"Hey, I was just doing my job—keeping you safe, watching your back. That's what an undercover leg man does. Taylor Street is still part of the department even though it doesn't exist. What flavor Gatorade do you like?"

"How about you tell us, Johnny?"

Johnny smiled to show off his gold-starred tooth. "Lola likes mango ... and Frankie, you like ... rye."

JULY 24, 2006/7:00 P.M.
CHICAGO, THE CITY OF BIG BALLS

THE POLICE SOFTBALL LEAGUE played at a number of parks around the city. Chicago softball is played with a sixteen-inch ball called a "Clincher." It is hard as a rock, but men don't wear gloves when they play. All softball junkies have crooked fingers from catching Clinchers. First-aid kits filled with Popsicle sticks and rolls of white tape are kept on every team bench. When players break a finger, they simply tape a Popsicle stick to the broken finger, like a splint, and wrap it to a good finger for support.

Lola played in a co-ed police league and the women were allowed to wear gloves. Most of the women had played fast pitch (twelve-inch softballs) in high school and brought the tradition of wearing gloves into the slow-pitch league. Lola had played shortstop on an Illinois championship high school girls' team and never threw like a girl. The fact of the matter was, she had a gun

27

for an arm. I wondered if Johnny knew Lola also kept a handgun in her softball duffel bag. As I watched Lola warm up, I knew she wasn't going to have a good game. The descent into the gravel pit had sapped the juices out of her body. In the third inning, she got a bad cramp in her calf while running to first base and pulled up lame; so she decided to call it quits for the night.

She climbed into my Oldsmobile 442, and we headed back to our virtual office. Our new place was a seven-room house. It was hard changing living accommodations every few weeks or days, but it was a necessary evil. If we stayed put too long, somebody who didn't like us might eventually find us, and then we might have to kill them because nobody except a criminal would come looking for us. Some weeks we lived in a place that was a dump; other weeks, we stayed in a fancy hotel room. But we never stayed for long and the police gave us new plates for our cars every week. This week, my Olds sported Arkansas plates from a traveling salesman's car because he got put in jail for soliciting sex with an undercover policewoman at a gentleman's club south of the airport. What he whispered into the policewoman's ear wasn't very gentlemanly, so the department figured he wouldn't need his license plates for a while.

I could tell Lola wasn't in a talkative mood. She was too busy working the cramp out of her calf. Lola has really nice legs, and me watching her massaging her leg while I was driving was probably more dangerous than me text-messaging with both thumbs while driving. When she finally got the cramp to subside, she reached into the glove box and pulled out a cell phone. She held it up for me to see. "Look what I found."

"A cell phone. Cool. Why don't you see if you can figure out how to call the owner? You might get a reward for returning it."

"I don't think so. The battery's dead."

"Well, then toss it."

"I don't think so."

"Why?"

"My intuition tells me the owner is dead too."

That surprised me so much I drove right through a red light. If you drive through a red light in Chicago, a camera takes a picture of the license plate and the car owner automatically gets a very expensive ticket for a moving violation. Thanks to me, the traveling salesman from Arkansas was in for another surprise. When I regained my composure, I asked Lola, "What makes you think the owner of the cell phone is dead?"

"I found it at the bottom of the quarry."

"On your nature hike?"

"I wasn't taking a nature hike. I was looking for clues. I figured while you were jawing with Johnny Rice, I might come across something. And I did. When we get home, we can recharge the battery and see if this phone might have any-thing to do with our new case. What did you and Johnny talk about?"

"Mostly the White Sox relief pitching."

"And what did you learn?"

"Something I always knew: my partner is more on the ball than me ... or the White Sox."

Lola smiled and began rubbing my leg, which was always a good sign.

JULY 24, 2006/8:35 P.M.
AN UNDERGROUND PASSAGE TO
AN ABOVE-BOARD SAFEHOUSE

I PARKED THE OLDSMOBILE in a warehouse in Bridgeport and we took an underground passage from
the warehouse into the basement of the house that
was to be our new home away from home. We
noted it had a foreclosed sign in the front yard. In
the summer of 2006, the nation's failing economy
claimed homes from many families. Real estate
prices and the stock market plunged. The front
and back doors of this house were padlocked from
the outside so we weren't worried about anybody
breaking in. Since the house was in the mayor's
old neighborhood, the Taylor Street Widows' and
Orphans' Fund purchased the house as an invest-
ment and began to renovate it for future use.

The first thing we did when we got inside
was turn the air-conditioning on high. Then we
took a shower together, another good sign. Conservation of water is always a good thing during

31

Chicago's hottest months. But when Lola turned the cold water on full blast, it was her way of telling me she wasn't in the mood for anything except a shower. The cold water felt great—we both had had enough heat for one day—but taking a cold shower is always hard on a guy's manhood; so that ensured no hanky-panky tonight.

Truthfully, the cold shower took the starch out of me. So when I crawled into bed next to Lola, all I was capable of doing was making small talk. "Johnny told me we don't meet this girl we'll be babysitting for a couple more days," I said. "We're going to a place called Pleasant Ridge, so I think it's going to be light duty. Ever hear of Pleasant Ridge?"

Lola smirked and said, "Pleasant Ridge? Are you kidding me, Frankie? Don't you ever read police memos? Pleasant Ridge is where they relocate witnesses who were involved in cases involving the most violent crimes."

I was stunned. "Are you kidding me?"

Lola smiled back. "Yes, I am! Boy, I got you good. It serves you right for not reading the whole assignment letter."

"Wow, you really had me psyched up. I was ready to exchange a little lead with some bad guys."

"We're not going to Pleasant Ridge. That's the town where the nearest post office is."

"Then where are we going?"

"We are going to Edensgate, 'The Farm of the Future.'"

"Oh, goody, goody! I've sat in traffic jams for hours on the Edens Expressway, so I'm guessing it isn't going to be paradise."

Lola continued, "I read a story about it in the paper a few months ago. It's nowhere near the Edens Expressway. William G. Edens was an Illinois politician who sponsored the first bond issue for paved roads in Chicago. But, Edensgate Farm is over two hundred miles west of Chicago, and it is way bigger than the town of Pleasant Ridge.

"In our assignment letter—that you didn't read—it says we're going to the Farm of the Future because the rich people who own the farm have a thirteen-year-old daughter who has been training a racehorse, and the stable thinks it is going to be a really, really good one. So, they have been training it on this farm so nobody will know about it and how fast it is.

"It's not like somebody is going to kidnap this girl and hold her for ransom. They just want to keep the horse and the fact that a thirteen-year-old girl is training it under wraps. So, what did Johnny Rice tell you about the dead jockey? How does he fit into the picture?"

"He didn't tell me anything. He just wanted to meet us. He's the department's leg man at the racetracks, legal, and illegal betting establishments. There's always something illegal going on. It might not have anything to do with our job. But, then again, it might. So, he just wanted to keep us in the loop. Do you want to get up early and go out for breakfast?"

"No, I'm still burping up beef and *giardiniera*. So, if you didn't talk about the dead jockey, what exactly did you two talk about for two hours?"

"Guy stuff. In addition to the Astro van, Johnny has a midnight-blue Barracuda with blue neon lights under the floor pan."

"Why would somebody put blue neon lights under a Barracuda?"

"It makes the Barracuda look like it's swimming in water. Cool, huh?"

"Frankie, when I open the door of the refrigerator, it lights up inside. Is that cool, too?"

"Of course not; the light isn't blue."

Lola didn't laugh. "Did you get any information about the jockey?"

"Like how the jockey got dead?" I paused for maximum dramatic effect. "My guess is ... he couldn't swim."

"Thanks for reminding me, Frankie."

"About what?"

"Speaking of the dead ..." Lola got out of bed and plugged in the cell phone. "Hopefully the dead battery of the cell phone I found will be charged by morning and, hopefully, we will be able to find out something about this case."

Then she got back in bed, turned out the

lights, and fell asleep right away. I must have been pretty tired, too, because I don't remember falling asleep. Some nights I am so tired when I get in bed, I just black out and don't dream. It seems when that happens, I wake up feeling really good. But if I am working on a case, I don't sleep well. Instead I find myself walking the streets of Chicago looking for clues in my dreams. After those nights, I wake up tired.

Tonight I first fell into a black sleep, but then I must have started dreaming because something way in the back of my mind was bothering me about our new case. Being bodyguards for a thirteen-year-old girl was pretty easy duty. Anytime the money is too easy, somebody is holding something back. But, instead of waking up, I dreamed I woke up inside my dream, but, I didn't know where I was because I woke up in complete darkness in my dream. It bothered me because I couldn't see a thing. It was kind of creepy. Then I heard someone strike a stick match behind me. I turned and saw a dark-skinned man lighting a cigarette. He wore an old-fashioned suit, and he looked me right in the eye and shook his head like he didn't approve of me and how I was approaching the case. Then he blew out the match, and I woke up. In spite of the cold shower and the air-conditioning being on full blast, I was soaked in sweat. It was dawn.

At first I thought I was dead because I saw an

angel in a cloud at the foot of the bed. It turned out I was looking at the backside of Lola who stood naked while she smoked a cigarette. She was messing with the cell phone she had found.

I cleared my voice to get her attention. "Did it take a charge?"

"No. We might need to take it to the police station and see if Danny can get a techie to do something with it."

"Why did you get up so early?"

"I couldn't sleep. You seemed to be having a nightmare."

"I'm sorry. Did I wake you?"

"Yes." She gave up on the cell phone. "Do you have any idea whose house this was?"

"No. Why?"

"I don't know. I'm getting a very bad vibe from this place. What in the world is going on, Frankie? A few weeks ago, a family was living in this house. I went into the kids' bedrooms. The family who used to live here has an eight-year-old boy and a ten-year-old girl. This was their house. We just slept in their parents' bed. I feel awful, like I do when I know something I did is very wrong. Why should we be able to walk in here like we own the place and sleep in their bed? Those people should have slept here last night, not us. Why did they have to leave? Where did they go? Why couldn't they just stay here? What's the bank going to do with this house and all their stuff?"

"There's a lot of that going on, Lola. I gotta think we were pretty lucky getting assigned to Taylor Street when we did. Otherwise, we might be living on the street right now. We should be grateful that we landed on our feet."

"Actually we landed in somebody else's bed. Remind me again why we got divorced."

"We weren't happy. We got tired of our routine. We felt tied down. Our life wasn't exciting. And we were both in counseling for anger management issues. We weren't thinking clearly. So, we stopped talking to each other and began talking to our lawyers instead. We hired lawyers to think and talk for us, and they decided it would be a good idea if we got a divorce. Then, we sold our house at a loss, and the lawyers took all of our money."

Lola thought about it for a minute. "Well, live and learn." Lola took a long drag on her cigarette and let it out very slowly. Then she looked at me and said, "Frankie, I have a confession to make to you. When I signed the divorce papers, I crossed my fingers … so it didn't count; we're not divorced."

I smiled at her and said, "That's good to know. That's very good to know."

WHO ORDERED DEAD DUCK ON BROWN RICE?

SINCE WE HAD THE day off, we decided to go to the police station to see our buddy and benefactor, Captain Danny Doyle. We owed Danny a lot for getting us into Taylor Street. When we walked into his office, he wasn't happy to see us. "Where in the world have you two been? We've been looking for you since yesterday morning."

I answered, "We went to the post office to get our assignment out of the post office box; where we met Johnny Rice. He took us to lunch at Novi's, and then he drove us to the stone quarry in Stickney."

Danny just shook his head. "I don't think so. Johnny Rice has been lying on a slab in the morgue for three days."

"What?" Lola and I said together.

Danny continued, "Johnny was killed the night before last."

Lola and I were stunned. "How could that be? We saw him yesterday."

Danny motioned for us to sit in the two chairs in front of his desk, and he continued his story. "Two patrolmen pulled Johnny's body out of a dipsy-dumpster a couple of blocks away from the post office in an alley off Erie. The garbage men saw a leg sticking out of the dipsy-dumpster and called us. Detective Johnny Rice got his throat slit. It took us some time to identify him because his ID and badge were not on his person. So there was no way you two could have eaten lunch with Johnny."

I quickly put two and two together. "I'm guessing we ate lunch with the guy that killed Johnny Rice. The badge he flashed at us was real; so we didn't ask to see his ID."

Lola scowled. "That means we ate lunch with a killer. How does a guy have balls big enough to pull off something like that? He must have a heart made of granite. No wonder he took us to a rock quarry."

Then Danny asked, "What did the guy look like?"

I described him as best I could. "He was built like a boxer: lanky, tall, coffee-colored skin. He had a front tooth that was gold except for a star shape in the enamel. He was dressed like a homeless guy. When we went into the post office,

I thought he was a scam artist because he had a wheelchair that made it look like he didn't have any legs. When we came out, he was standing and waiting for us."

Danny said, "Your first instinct was correct." Danny reached into his desk drawer and pulled out a file. "This is a picture of Johnny Rice. As you can clearly see, he was a short, one-legged man of Chinese descent." I was thinking fast. The guy we met probably did something to Johnny and then wheeled him off in his wheelchair so he could kill him. Erie Street was only a couple of blocks from the post office. Danny told us Johnny worked that neighborhood undercover for years, digging dirt from the homeless who lived in flophouse hotels when they had money and Lower Wacker Drive when they didn't, until the Mayor permanently shagged them out of their winter shelter beneath the city. Nobody ever suspected Johnny Rice was an undercover cop until a couple of days ago.

Lola was quick to speak up. "So, what the hell happened? Why was he killed?"

Danny put the file back into his drawer. "Your guess is as good as mine. He must have come across some information he wasn't supposed to. Anyway, the guy who killed Johnny must be working for someone. What little we know so far, he's a player. He played the two of you and the county coroner like a pro. He thought out all the angles. He called McGoonin because the body of the jockey was in an unincorporated area. When I heard about what happened to Johnny, I put out an alert, especially since his badge and ID were missing. McGoonin didn't read the alert until after he had fished the jockey out of the water. When he read it, he remembered the name and put two and two together. Then he contacted me and said Johnny Rice had slipped through his fingers. He also said Johnny Rice had two detectives with him who matched your descriptions and asked if you were legit. McGoonin is a pretty sharp guy."

Lola smiled and asked, "What did you tell him?"

"You know I always got your backs. I'm not sure what this is all about, but the guy that killed Johnny took a big chance using his badge. He must have really done his homework to pull this thing off. My guess is he killed the jockey, too, and used the time he spent with you to get more information about the security job guarding the kid. What did you tell him?"

Lola held her hands up in mock surrender. "Don't look at me. Frankie did all the talking with the guy with the gold tooth." Lola fish-eyed me to let me know it was my turn to talk.

So, I told Danny what I knew. "All I did was pick up the package out of the post office box. I read it …"

Lola quickly interrupted. "Frankie skimmed it. *I* read it in detail."

I picked up where Lola left off. "After Lola read the letter, she gave it back to me, and I put it in my pocket. I never showed it to the guy or talked to him about it. In all honesty, there isn't any real information in it." I reached into my pocket and pulled out the letter. "Here it is. Read it for yourself." I placed the envelope on the desk.

Danny opened it and read. "All you really got is a name and an address. As far as the horse and the girl go, who knows? The horse has never raced yet, and how good can a thirteen-year-old trainer be? This isn't the kind of information you kill somebody for. My guess is the guy knew all that stuff before you did. So, Frankie, what did you talk about with this guy?"

"The usual. Baseball. Women. Cars. Interesting murders and mutilations. You know, cop talk."

Lola frowned and said, "I'm a cop, and I don't talk about women. While the boys were talking shop, I did some real police work." Lola put the cell phone she found on Danny's desk. "I found this cell phone in the bottom of the quarry. I figured it might have fallen out of somebody's pocket when the jockey was being dumped into the drink. I recharged the battery last night, but I can't get it to work. Can your CSI team make magic and get it to work?"

Danny laughed. "These days we're so short-handed we're lucky if we have enough people to answer the phone much less fix a dead phone to find information. But, I'll see what I can do."

"So, now what do we do?" I asked.

"You tell me. You're the only ones who know what this guy looks like. If there is even a slim chance this guy is out to hurt the kid or the horse, you two might be the best ones to keep them out of harm's way. But, I also completely understand if you don't want to take this assignment."

Lola and I exchanged looks, and she spoke before I could. "I think we need to take it to protect ourselves. This guy posed as an undercover cop, and it seemed like he knew everything about us. He knew I liked mango Gatorade and Frankie liked rye. That really pissed me off. My vote is to take the job and find out everything there is to know about this creep … and then let nature take its course. If we find him, then we can prosecute him for pretending to be a cop. Frankie?"

I replied, "Since it's two against one, I think the odds favor us. Who knows, this might be fun. An opportunity might arise where I get to shoot him. The police department still frowns upon criminals impersonating police officers, right Danny?"

"Absolutely. And if either of you shoots him in self-defense, we would not have a problem with that."

We all shook hands. Then Lola and I went out to the parking lot, got into my Olds, turned onto the Eisenhower Expressway, and headed to the land west of Chicago, to where they keep the horses. Since we always have overnight bags packed away in the trunk, we left town on a moment's notice to meet our new employer. The Olds has a really big trunk, and we always carry a good selection of firearms, weapons, body bags, and an ample supply of mango Gatorade and rye. So, we are always good to go.

JULY 25, 2006/11:22 A.M.

GIVE AN INCH TO
GET PAST THE PINCH

NO MATTER WHAT DAY of the week it is, no matter
what time of the day it is, the traffic on the
Eisenhower Expressway heading west out of Chicagoland is murder. And road rage is the norm.
For some reason, as you leave the congestion of the
city, just before you reach the wide-open spaces of
the west side, the expressway narrows. With all
the empty space available on the west side, why
that happens is one of the great unsolved mysteries of Chicago. Everybody speeds up as they drive
toward the pinch in the road—and every day they
have a NASCAR Talladega "Big One." (If you're
not a NASCAR fan, Talladega Superspeedway is
famous for final-lap, high-speed accidents that
destroy most of the cars that are left in the race.)
On a major city freeway, it is equally exciting. One
day, as I approached the pinch, several teenagers
who were joyriding in a small car bounced off

a concrete wall and slid their car under a semi-trailer which turned sideways trying to avoid the car. The semi skidded at least a city block, blocking all the lanes, and it stopped just short of slamming into the car full of teenagers. But, it stopped off-balance at a precarious angle, and it teetered on edge for what seemed like an eternity, and then it fell over, crushing the carful of kids as flat as a pancake. I was still a cop at the time, and it happened right in front of me, so I pulled up next to the truck and tried to calm down the driver who thought he crushed a carful of kids. I told him I saw the whole thing happen, and it wasn't his fault. The driver was disoriented, but I got him to crawl back into the cab and turn off the truck engine. Once the engine was off, we could hear the kids inside the little car screaming and yelling for help. It turned out they all survived without a scratch. Each time I drive past the pinch, I think of them. The accident closed the Eisenhower Expressway for four hours and backed traffic up to Iowa.

Once Lola and I drove past the pinch, we were in the real Illinois. Chicago is urban; the rest of Illinois is rural. It is a state of opposites united by a common flatness. Illinois is flat like nowhere else is flat. The highest point in Chicago is only twelve feet above the lowest point. That area is on the south side of Chicago in an area known as Beverly Hills. As you drive past the highest point in Chicago, they have a plaque designating the location as the highest point in the city. There is a suburb of Chicago called Mount Prospect, but it is as flat as the rest of the state. In July, as you head west out of the city, the most notable change is that the landscape becomes very green with farm crops. There are some trees, but mostly it is mile after mile of farmland. The population outside of Chicago proper is about equal to the population of Chicago. Anyone from out of state who vacations in Illinois goes to Chicago. But if you live in Chicago, most residents explore the rest of the state at least once on a family vacation. Lola and I never went on a family vacation to see Illinois as kids, so this was our once-in- a-lifetime chance to see the flatlands and see how the other half of the state lived.

JULY 25, 2006/3:15 P. M.
FLATLANDERS AND CORN MAZES

ONCE WE WERE OUT of Chicagoland, the drive took us about four hours. Like most Illinois highways, the scenery as you drive west is similar to the scenery you see if you drive south or east or north. Illinois scenery is redundant. If you don't like change, the scenery could be called reliable, but if you want a change of scenery, you have to go back to Chicago. One sight of interest we saw was a very long diesel-powered freight train hauling coal north to Wisconsin to make electricity. Believe it or not, there is a lot of coal underneath Illinois, and it has always been an important part of the state's economy. Most people think of West Virginia or Pennsylvania when they think of coal mining. But, Illinois is also a big producer of coal.

Ironically, Illinois spent countless dollars developing nuclear power plants to reduce the burning of coal, but in recent years, the Zion nuclear power plant was taken out of use. Nuclear waste disposal became a political issue and a bio-hazard. Disposing of it properly was expensive. So, it was disposed of improperly, which eventually made it even more expensive. And nuclear waste can be more hazardous than burning coal. As they say, sometimes the devil you know is better than the one that you don't. Maybe putting coal into kids' Christmas stockings might eventually become a positive thing.

Primarily, Illinois is a farming state. As the miles rolled by, we saw mile after mile of cornfields. Since it was late July, the corn was past knee-high as in "knee-high by the Fourth of July." Our destination was Edensgate Farm. Even though it was gaining a statewide reputation as The Farm of the Future, there were no billboards advertising. I guess our client valued privacy more than tourists. It was well off the beaten path, hidden among mazes of cornfields that all looked alike on roads that weren't on maps. During the mid-1800s the federal government began to encourage farmers to head west. Many of the immigrant farmers thought they had died and went to heaven when they reached the flat lands of Illinois. Many bought as much land as they could afford. Farms were separated by country roads that defined each farm's boundaries. The roads were "eleven rods wide" so ox carts could pass each other. These days, the roads were wide enough so that John Deere tractors (which are made in Peoria, Illinois) could pass each other. There was no standard size or shape for farms; the roads just sort of meandered. If you asked a local for directions, good luck. They lived in the maze, and they had a second sense of where everything was. Tourists should never wander off the interstate in rural Illinois to take scenic routes that were not on the roadmaps unless they had a full tank of gas, because if they got lost in the endless maze of corn they might end up in Kansas just like Dorothy did.

I wasn't worried about getting lost because Lola was a great navigator and the directions we were given were excellent. When we came upon Edensgate, The Farm of The Future, it did not look like any other farm in the state. It looked like something Disney World would have built at Epcot to present the perfect farm of the future. All around the perimeter of the farm were fancy, new, white windmills with airplane-like propellers. Seventy years ago, a single windmill was a common sight on most farms. It was also a necessity on a farm if a family wanted electricity to light a house at night or to listen to a ballgame on the radio. Edensgate had enough windmills to power a small town. The windmills towered above miles and miles of traditional, white wooden fence that surrounded the farm to keep its livestock from wandering.

Edensgate had gained a reputation as a stud farm where thoroughbred racehorses of note were bred and trained. There were lots of grassy pastures with trees. Late July is the prettiest time to see farms in Illinois. The fields and grasses were a rich green and the white fences looked like gigantic picture frames creating pastoral land-scapes. You don't see a lot of pretty white fences in Chicago. Chicagoans are a more practical in their choice of fences; chain-link seems to be the inner city "de-fence" of choice if you want to keep intruders out. In the case of Edensgate, I think the goal was to keep the animals in. Maybe it was the Tom Sawyer in me, but when I looked at the white fence, it made me smile ... because I thought of the poor sucker who had to paint it. However, in the case of Edensgate, I'd bet the farm was one place in the state where there was no unemploy-ment for able-bodied painters.

THE GUARDS AT
EDENSGATE ARE NO ANGELS

EDENSGATE FARM HAD A beautiful entrance gate. When I was a kid, my dad told me about a television cowboy named Roy Rogers. Dad said Roy Rogers was his hero because Roy Rogers was a good guy who wore a white hat who fought bad guys who wore black hats. Dad said it was easy for kids to tell the good guys from the bad guys on black-and-white televisions. Roy Rogers owned a ranch called "The Double Bar R" and its gate was always open to everyone—but things are more complicated these days. The bad guys aren't as easy to spot. And so, Edensgate's gate was always closed and visitors had to stop at a security building to check in with two armed guards. To me, this was a clue that this was definitely not an ordinary farm.

The security guard who greeted us was pleasant, in a military kind of way. It was obvious he took great pride in his appearance, like a Marine does when he wears his dress uniform. His name tag read "McDonald."

"Welcome to Edensgate Farm, sir," he said. "Can I have two forms of identification from each of you? I need to check to see if your names are on our visitor roster." I handed him my driver's license and private investigator's license from my wallet, and Lola got hers out of her fanny pack. He handed them to his partner, who logged all the information into a computer. The computer happily chirped when our names appeared on the approved visitor roster. He said our names aloud as he returned our identification cards to us so there would be no mistake of who was who. Then he asked me to open the trunk. Since my 442 was built before automatic trunk releases, I told him I'd have to get out of the car to open it with a key. McDonald said he would prefer I give him my keys; so I did. When he opened the trunk, he drew his side arm and asked us both to get out of the car with our hands over our heads. Obviously he had spotted our arsenal of weapons, stash of extra ammunition, and hand grenades. Then he asked if either of us were carrying firearms or any other concealed weapons on our persons. When we said yes, he looked even more shocked.

I asked permission to speak so I could bring him up to speed. He granted it to me; so I spoke.

"We are private investigators who have been hired by Mr. Clay Spangler to act as bodyguards for his daughter. We were told to bring whatever equipment we deemed necessary to ensure her safety. Perhaps you should contact him."

"Do you have permits for all these weapons?"

"Of course."

McDonald looked concerned, scared, and worried all at the same time; but to his credit, he didn't break his security protocol. His partner made the call. To their amazement, we got approval to enter our fingerprints into their security system for confirmation of our identities. I wasn't sure what kind of sense of humor this kid had—or if he even had one—so I avoided the temptation of asking him if he wanted to do a retinal scan and a cavity check too.

Once we were approved, I complimented McDonald on his adherence to company procedures and protocol. We shook hands, and then he introduced us to his partner, Abigail Brown, who introduced herself as a former MP who just returned from Iraq. Abigail Brown had red hair and plenty of freckles. She stood six feet tall and weighed in at around 200 pounds; I'm guessing she was a pretty capable MP. We all agreed that we were happy to help each other in any way possible. McDonald handed me a map of Edensgate with a red line of the route we were to follow to reach our guest accommodations. We were asked not to deviate from the path until after we were given a tour.

As I drove, Lola studied the map and fed me tidbits of information. "Frankie, this place is 7,500 acres. They raise organic foods here. Even the livestock is fed with organic feed. They are an energy-independent farm. They grow corn to make E85, and their windmills produce enough electricity to sell it to the local electric company. So, the farm makes a profit from the windmills, and they never need to buy gasoline. They have ten thoroughbred horses in training on the premises. What more could you ask for?"

"Do they have a tavern?"

Lola ignored my snappy repartee.

"Where are we going to bunk tonight?" I asked.

"Bunk? Wow, five minutes on the farm and you've gone rustic on me. But, if they do have bunkbeds, I've got the top." She pointed to a college dorm-like building. "I think that's it. We've got the Lincoln Suite. It's not made out of logs, pardner, but it has a cement pond in back, in case we want to take a dip."

"Lola, I think you're right. I'm starting to wonder if this is a job or a vacation. We're being paid to hang out with a thirteen-year-old girl."

"You don't see me complaining, do you? Relax! This is going to be like working security at a theme park except we can enjoy the attractions."

Lola pointed as she spoke, "Take a right at the next corner and enter the parking lot."

I pulled the Olds into our designated parking space. Out of habit, we decided to case the place so we knew what was what and what was where. We made note of all the security systems for the building and other electrical lines that were connected to the building. These days, a really good thief can hide his wires among the utility wires.

When we went inside, we did the same. We noted where the wires were that connected us to the security building at the main gate, in case we wanted to cut the wires to let them know who was in charge. We were sure they'd pay us a visit if we did. Then we hid and secured our weapons. When we checked out the kitchen, we found a very nice organic fruit basket for us. All the whole-grain goodies were made right here on the farm. We also found a note on the kitchen table that requested our presence in the main house as soon as we were settled. So we obliged.

JULY 25, 2006/5:10 P.M.
WHO YOU CALLING
HORSE TRAINERS?

AFTER THE LONG DRIVE, we decided to stretch our legs and walk. We hadn't walked very far, when we heard the honk of a Jeep horn behind us. The driver pulled up next to us and stopped. Behind the steering wheel was a teenage girl dressed in a dirty t-shirt, blue jeans spattered with mud, and rubber boots. For a young girl, she seemed very self-assured and cordially introduced herself. "Hi, I'm Chita Spangler. Do you want a lift?"

We instantly realized that this was the girl we were hired to protect, but she dressed more like a field hand than a billionaire's daughter. She didn't wear makeup, she was dirty from head to toe, and her shirt was soaked with sweat from working hard. She was sort of plain, but she did have beautiful, long, brown hair; dark-green eyes; sun freckles on her nose; and nice straight teeth with braces. She wore a simple gold chain with a small gold medallion around her neck. She took off her work gloves and offered us her slender callused hand to shake.

I shook it first and said, "Sure, we'd like a ride. But, do you think you should be offering rides to two strangers? We might be hitchhikers for all you know."

Chita furled her brow. "What are hitchhikers?"

Lola and I wondered if she was serious. Obviously, she was; so we didn't press the issue. Lola then asked, "How old are you?"

"Thirteen."

"Have you got a driver's license?"

"No. I just drive around the farm. I've been driving for four years already."

Lola pulled out her badge. "I hate to tell you, but we're cops."

Chita looked alarmed. "You are? Am I in trouble?"

Lola smiled and said, "No. We're your bodyguards from Chicago."

Chita breathed a sigh of relief. "Wow. You could have fooled me!"

I corrected her. "We did fool you."

Chita laughed. "I guess you did. I thought you were the two new horse trainers my mom just hired. That's who usually stays in the Lincoln Suite. She must really like you. Only special guests get to stay in that suite. Wow! I've never met any police officers before."

"You're lucky," Lola cracked.

I quickly added, "But I can see how you mistook us for horse trainers. What's your favorite cop show on television?"

"We don't have cable out here, so I don't watch cop shows. Besides, I stay pretty busy all day. I was just heading home for dinner, so hop in. Don't worry, I'm a good driver. I never got a single ticket."

"That's because you've never met a cop," Lola said with a smile.

Lola and I got in the Jeep. Chita was a good driver as she worked through the manual gear box. As soon as she pulled into the driveway, a pack of beagles greeted her with bays and high-pitched barks of excitement and joy. As soon as Chita got out of the Jeep, they surrounded her, each one tumbling over the other trying to get her attention. She introduced us to her friends. "These are my beagles, Joe, Shirley, and Mary." As soon as they focused on us, their baying renewed and grew shriller. Lola squatted down and gave them attention, which quieted them down again. Chita said, "Joe has the blue collar. Shirley has the orange collar. And Mary has the green collar."

I finally chimed in, "Nobody is going to sneak up on you with that pack of beagle bedlam around you. They remind me of Moe, Curly, and Larry."

Chita frowned. "Are those policemen?"

I guessed she wasn't a *Three Stooges* fan.

A Border collie calmly walked up behind Chita and sat next to her. She petted him on the head. "This is my police dog—even though he's a Border collie. We call him Sheriff because he keeps Joe, Shirley, and Mary in check. He also herds the sheep, and he is my horse's best friend. He is really smart. He just sits and watches most of the time. But if he sees something he doesn't like, he takes charge." Chita pointed at Lola and said, "Sheriff, go introduce yourself."

Sheriff sauntered over to us with the casual confidence and swagger of John Wayne. He was polite and shook Lola's hand first. Then he walked over to me. He smelled me a little and looked back at Chita with a baleful look. She told him, "He's okay." He turned around and offered his paw to me. I shook it; he wagged his tail. Chita knew things were under control. Since the dogs were behaving, Chita turned on a hose so she could start washing off her rubber boots. "I was mucking stalls so I have to hose off my boots. Mom doesn't like me to track muck in the house. I guess you know what muck is, right?" We nodded our heads in unison. "Follow Sheriff to the house. We don't lock the doors, so just go in the back door and shout out for my mom. Her name is Marguerite. She's in there somewhere. If you can't find her, Sheriff will."

Sheriff stood up and did exactly what Chita told him to; the beagles stayed behind with Chita.

When we got to the back door, I opened it without knocking. It felt odd, but Lola and I walked inside as if we were lifelong neighbors. I guess that's what they call "neighborly" in the country. In Chicago, we call it "breaking and entering," but I felt okay about doing it since Sheriff was with us. We shouted out, and instantly we heard the clatter of high heels on tile coming toward us. I figured a maid was coming to greet us but instead, a stunning, black-haired woman who dressed like a Spanish Jackie Kennedy greeted us. When she entered the kitchen, she looked a little confused to see us; but Sheriff walked up to her and wagged his tail letting her know we were friends. She said, "Hello, I'm Marguerite Martinez Spangler. Are you the new horse trainers?"

Chita entered just in time to hear her mother's question. "No, Mom, these are my bodyguards from Chicago. I thought they were horse trainers, too." Then she turned to introduce us, but realized she didn't know our names either, so we introduced ourselves.

"We're the bodyguards referred by the Chicago Police Department. I'm Frankie Turk, and this is Lola Lahti."

The stunningly beautiful woman extended her hand to shake ours. "Welcome to our home. Thank you for agreeing to help us. Please, pardon my accent. I am from Brazil. You have already met my daughter, Chita Thelma Spangler, and Sheriff.

My husband hired you as a precautionary measure. He has frequently been in the public eye of late, and we thought it would be wise to increase security around our daughter."

"I am training a horse that is very special," Chita said with pride. "His name is Dandyosa."

I asked, "What kind of horse is Dandyosa?"

"Dandyosa is a thoroughbred stallion. He is descended from a long line of champions, and he was bred and born right here on the farm. I helped deliver him when I was ten and watched him being born. He is going to race his first race soon. He is very, very fast. Would you like to see him?"

Her mother interrupted. "Chita, there will be time for that tomorrow. Let me spend some time with our guests."

Chita looked crestfallen; so I said, "I promise we'll do it first thing tomorrow morning, Chita. I love horses." That made her happy, and she went upstairs to her room.

Her mother invited us into the den.

PAINTED HORSES
OF DIFFERENT COLORS

AN OLD GRANDFATHER CLOCK chimed six times as we entered the den of the Spangler Mansion. The walls were filled with original oil paintings of racehorses. As I looked at the paintings, I realized I had won money betting on some of them. Marguerite offered us a drink, but we refused since we were on duty.

"I want to thank you for accepting our offer," said Marguerite. "You will be paid in cash, as we agreed. Your presence is primarily a precautionary measure. We have ample security, but I only have one daughter and these days a person can't be too safe. Because of the economy, too, many people have become desperate. Too many people have too little, and a few people have too much. Money is in short supply, and my husband is constantly in the news with his oil company. As the oil prices rise, the public gets angrier. Everyone who works here is happy. We pay our employees well. Our farm is not in the public spotlight, and our energy conservation efforts are applauded by our neighbors. There is not much to do on the farm. But I want you to know, the time you spend on the farm will only be a few weeks. That time will be spent getting to know Chita. Your real work will take place when we move Dandyosa to Cicero at the end of the summer. Chita hopes to run Dandyosa at the Gold Stakes Race on Labor Day weekend."

Lola asked, "Won't Chita be in school by then?"

"No," answered Marguerite. "Chita is home-schooled. Her tutors will travel with her, and she will keep up with her studies. Chita is very focused for a thirteen-year-old. She knows she must do well with her school work to be able to continue to train her horse. She has her heart set on Dandyosa winning the Gold Stakes Cup."

I pointed at one of the paintings. "If I'm not mistaken, this horse, Chilly Too Hot, won the Gold Stakes Cup ten years ago."

"You are correct. So, you are a racing fan, Mr. Turk?"

"Just a casual fan. Do you think Dandyosa has a chance?"

"Chita has a way with animals. And she loves that horse. All horses love to run, and they respond well to love. But, with horses, you never know. That's what makes a horse race interesting."

"What makes you think Chita might be in danger?" asked Lola.

"As I said, my husband is always in the news. He is a Texas oil man, and he knows how to make deals and friends and ... sometimes enemies. Recently he had some trouble while he was abroad, and he will be returning home soon. So, adding a little extra security seemed like a smart precautionary measure."

Lola asked another question. "Why does a Texas oil man have a farm in Illinois?"

Marguerite smiled and confessed, "I am very persuasive. I met Clay at a thoroughbred sale in Argentina fifteen years ago. We both went there to bid on the same horse. He recognized my family name and knew my father made a fortune raising sugarcane for the production of ethanol. It helped turn Brazil's economy around. He became interested in my father's success. He outbid me for the horse, and I thought I would never see him again. But, two weeks later, the horse was shipped to our family plantation in Brazil as a present for me. He asked if he could see me again on his next trip to Brazil on the pretense that he could meet my father and gain some insights into the production of ethanol. I agreed. It turned out his real interest was me, and it also turned out he could be as persuasive as I was. Soon our relationship developed. At first we lived in Texas, but it was too hot and dry there for me. As a little girl, I often wondered what it would be like to live in a place where there were four seasons instead of one. I have a confession to make: after living in warm places most of my life, I have learned to love snow! I think it is beautiful! When I was a little girl, my father and mother visited Chicago in the winter, and they bought me a beautiful snow globe from Marshall Field's department store. I still have the snow globe and even the box it came in! So, Clay and I discussed building a home someplace far away from our family homes and making it a special place for us. We bought this wonderful piece of land and built a dream world."

Marguerite's story floored Lola. All she could say was, "Wow!"

I added, "That is an amazing story."

Marguerite continued. "I wanted to do something different and creative. Life is about change and moving forward. I love nature, and I studied biology and botany in college. I saw an opportunity here, like my father saw in Brazil. But, the state has a big problem. No one in Illinois wants to be a leader. The politicians promise jobs, but they don't say how they will create them. They want to reduce taxes, and at the same time, provide people with more services. But, that does not make any sense. They want to make the state better, but they don't want to change a thing."

I couldn't resist adding, "And they take up a lot of the space in state jails."

Marguerite laughed. "I agree. Many politicians go to jail in this state. But, I do what I can to help make Illinois better. Our farm is a productive start. We are profitable. We are energy efficient. We follow green guidelines. We generate so much electricity from wind and sun that we sell our excess electricity to the local electric company. We grow so much corn and sugarcane, we make enough ethanol to run our vehicles and sell the excess to the farmers around us at half the price they pay at gas stations. We also grow only organic fruits and vegetables. Even Dandyosa eats healthy food. I want everyone to be aware of Illinois' most famous natural resource."

"Coal?" I guessed.

Marguerite shook her head no and said, "Wind! People overlook wind because it is free. They don't call Chicago 'The Windy City' for nothing. The open prairies of the Illinois flatlands are very windy too."

"You should run for governor," said Lola.

Marguerite laughed. "The job of governor in Illinois is not a good one. In recent memory, three governors have gone to jail and another brazenly defies common sense. I prefer to lead by example. We are successful and different; so, there are some in the state capitol who oppose our efforts and attempt to set up roadblocks. A lawsuit was filed recently to shut down our windmills because they are unsightly."

"You're kidding?" I said.

"Lawyers will do anything to make a dollar or create a self-serving headline."

I smiled. "I think we're going to like working with you. We think the same way you do. We do whatever it takes to get the job done."

"Please excuse me," said Marguerite, "I am sorry but I have to take this phone call. It seems that our horse trainers missed their flight."

Our first meeting with our new employer was a great success. We saw eye to eye on a lot of things. Lola and I walked back from the Spangler's mansion to the Lincoln Suite feeling optimistic. Since times were so tough in the State of Illinois, it felt good to be optimistic for a change. We looked forward to getting a great night's sleep on The Farm of the Future.

A DEAD CELL PHONE
REVEALS A LIVE SUSPECT

MARGUERITE WALKED US OVER to the Lincoln Suite. "My husband met a very good horse trainer in Mexico and sent him and his favorite jockey to me to see if they would work well with Chita. I don't know why they haven't shown up yet. I don't like people who aren't punctual."

Lola suggested that maybe their flight was delayed or they took a wrong turn.

Marguerite replied, "I am a demanding employer. I always am fair if my employees are punctual and do a good job." She opened the door of the Lincoln Suite. "Since this suite is bigger and more luxurious, I will let you stay here. I'll call the maids and someone will check the trainer and his jockey into the Douglas Suite." Marguerite hesitated. "This is awkward. Can I assume you are married?"

I answered. "We got divorced a couple of

months ago, but our relationship is mending. We work together well, as cops. And we are working things out and making progress every day."

"Well, I can relate to your relationship. Clay and I have our differences too.

We'll have something to talk about. Let me know if you need anything. Breakfast is just before first light."

When my cell phone rang, it was Danny's number, so I called him back.

"Where are you, Frankie? What? No, hi? You need to keep your cell with you at all times."

"Lola and I arrived on time, at six. We parked my Olds, and we decided to stretch our legs after the long ride. But Chita picked us up in her Jeep and drove us to the Spangler house. I muted my phone because we were meeting the client and her daughter and I wanted to make a good first impression. I thought it would be rude to get a call in the middle of our first meeting, so I turned my phone off. Everything is fine here. It is a very low-pressure, relaxed place. Don't worry. We remembered to bring our guns. What's up?"

"The techies got the cell phone working that Lola found. It did belong to the floater. He was an apprentice jockey. He rode his first two races at a claimer track in Mexico. One horse went off at 80-1 and the other horse went off at 60-1."

"Let me guess. He won both by a mile."

"Exactly! And then he disappeared ... until he was found floating face down."

"I guess he pissed somebody off."

"Since this is out of Chicago's jurisdiction, I had to turn the cell phone over to the Illinois State Police. They'll handle the case from here. They called me late this afternoon and told me the jockey was of Mexican descent."

"I could have told you that by just looking at him."

"The State Police contacted the Tijuana Police Department. They've been very cooperative. No one reported the jockey missing. But, they did say he flew back to Chicago immediately after the races."

"After winning at those odds, I'd have done the same thing if I was him."

"His passport was legal, and he had been living in the U.S. But he did not ride any races in the U.S. Those two races in Tijuana were his first."

"And his last," I quipped.

"He was a groom at several stables, but they probably won't have much on him because he was just a peon. What I can't figure out is how a groom can learn to ride winners the first two times out."

"Maybe he wasn't a nobody like everybody thinks."

"You might be right, Frankie. But, the jockey had a video camera on his phone. We downloaded some very disturbing images before we turned the phone over to the State Police. If I send Detective Phillips out to you with the video, can you tell me if this is the man who led you to the jockey's body?"

"Sure. What was he doing when the jockey photographed him?"

"The man was shooting a racehorse in the head with a .357 Magnum."

JULY 26, 2006/5:00 A.M.
EARLY RISERS GET
BLUEBERRY MUFFINS

WHEN CHITA SAID SHE'D introduce us to Dandyosa first thing in the morning, she meant it. We thought first thing in the morning on a farm is when the sun starts to rise and the rooster crows. It's not. Lola and I were awakened before dawn by Chita's persistent knocking on our door. Lola answered it and had the presence of mind to be civil to Chita. I was impressed; her anger management classes were working. Lola even managed to smile when Chita asked, "Did I wake you?"

Lola asked if we could have five minutes to get dressed. She closed the door and both of us pulled on a pair of jeans and a t-shirt. We both wore shoulder holsters with guns so we'd look like bodyguards. Since it was July, the temperature was up to 90 degrees before the sun had a chance to shine. We ran out to Chita's Jeep, where she, Joe, Shirley, Mary, and Sheriff waited. It's nice to have four dogs shower you with affection before your first cup of coffee. Speaking of coffee, Chita had brought a thermos of coffee for us, and also a basket filled with blueberry muffins. I'm more of a bagel guy myself, but I figured I was at least a hundred and fifty miles from the nearest deli.

When we got to the stables, they were already a beehive of activity. There were ten horses in training at Edensgate Farm. When Chita drove up, an older man opened the door of the Jeep for her. Chita introduced him to us. "This is Pedro Diego. He manages the day-to-day operation of the stables." We all shook hands. Pedro was a short, well-weathered, older man who looked like he loved what he did and worked hard at it. Pedro excused himself because he had horses to get ready for early morning gallops. Sheriff fell in step at Chita's right side and the beagles rough-housed with each other but stayed with us.

Chita went straight to Dandyosa's stall. As soon as the black stallion saw her, he whinnied and was visibly excited to see her. If he didn't weigh over a thousand pounds, he would have probably wanted to sit in her lap like the beagles. Dandyosa's four black legs ended in four white socks. Those were the only white hairs on the entire horse. It looked like he was wearing spats. Dandyosa had the suave self-assurance of a young Sean Connery when he first played James

Bond. He walked right up to me and suddenly I felt like I was five years old again. I reached out and touched the soft hairs on his nose. He didn't move and neither did I. I smiled; he snorted; we bonded. It was hard to believe Dandyosa was a stallion owned and trained by a thirteen-year-old girl. Dandyosa must have really loved Chita because he let her braid pink, yellow, and purple ribbons into his mane and tail. I got the feeling the other horses wanted to laugh at Dandyosa, but they were afraid to. Dandyosa was definitely the alpha male at Edensgate Farm's stable.

Wild animals that run in herds pick leaders. They have an inbred sense of which animal is worth following. Dandyosa was a natural-born leader. Dandyosa displayed all the classic traits of a champion in maximum capacities. In thoroughbred racing, horses race in classes based on their dollar value. The most valuable horses are valuable because they can win against the best horses and against all odds. Just because one horse is faster than another horse, does not mean it will beat the other horse. That is the single factor that makes gambling on horses difficult. Horses have a social pecking order. As horses are raced in different groups, different leaders emerge. A horse that won several races against a lower class of racehorses might finish last against the next highest level of horses. It loses its confidence because it isn't comfortable. Most of the horses that train well enough to race can run similar times. As the purse levels go up, the herd is thinned by results.

The highest level of thoroughbred racing is a stakes race. Owners must stake a large sum of money to enter a horse in a stakes race. A stakes race is as much about the confidence of the owner as it is about the confidence of the horse. Races like the Kentucky Derby, the Preakness, and the Belmont are Grade I stakes races. Horses that have never won a race sometimes win those races, but it is a rare occurrence. The Gold Stakes is also a stakes race, so all of the horses have the best pedigrees. But, horses have good days and bad days just like people do. Some horses are moody and some are always the same. Sometimes "can't lose" betting favorites lose stakes races and an 80-1 longshot wins instead. Most horses are just horses, but every once in awhile a horse comes along that can comprehend more. Dandyosa was definitely aware he was special. When he walked through the barn, the other horses paid homage. I couldn't wait to see him on the track.

Once Dandyosa was on the track, it was hard to take my eyes off him. I had to keep reminding myself we were working, and our job was to ensure the safety of Chita. I needed to keep my edge and remain alert, but that was a difficult thing to do. I could not imagine someone breaking through Edensgate's security system and trying to kidnap or harm Chita or any of the horses.

Lola had run a check on of all the employ-ees. There were no strangers or new hires on the grounds. Chita was never alone. It seemed the three beagles were always around Chita, and each time someone new arrived, they would begin to bay like a bevy of canine burglar alarms. So, Lola and I didn't feel guilty we finally sat down to have our morning cups of coffee. There was a track behind the stalls. Lola and I took a posi-tion on the rail so we could watch. We kept our eyes glued on Chita as she galloped Dandyosa to warm him up. Dandyosa was raring to go, but he knew Chita was aboard and just warming him up for the jockey. The colt's coat was shiny and perfectly groomed. His ears perked forward. Each muscle in his body moved like liquid perfection as he took each stride. Chita and he were like one. He looked right at Lola and me before galloping off down to turn one.

A jockey dressed in his work clothes came up to us and introduced himself. "Hi, I'm Ramon Arroyo. Mrs. Spangler asked me to introduce myself to you." Ramon was a very famous jockey. He was from Argentina and was nearing the end of a great career. If you've never shaken hands with a jockey, it is an interesting experience. Most jockeys' hands are small, but they are as powerful as vise grips when they shake hands. Controlling a 900- to 1,100-pound thoroughbred racehorse takes two very strong hands. Ramon continued,

"I'll be riding Dandyosa in the Gold Stakes if he gets that far."

I smiled. "You have your doubts?"

Ramon shrugged. "Stranger things have happened. But this horse has never been on a track in front of people. He hasn't even run a maiden race yet. So, we have no idea what he might be capable of. Personally, I think he's going to be a real good one. But, most horses his age have already had a full year of racing. He's only raced against the horses here in the stables. Chita babies him. But, when I get on him, he's a whole lot of horse."

As Chita rode Dandyosa toward us, Ramon stepped out onto the track. Dandyosa was happy to see Ramon because he knew he was about to be turned loose. Ramon smiled when Dandyosa nudged his shoulder to get him aboard. Ramon helped Chita down and took her place, and they trotted off toward a starting gate. Some horses don't like getting into the starting gate, but Dandyosa knew it was his chance to run that morning, so he walked into it because he wanted to run. Chita took out her stopwatch. As the bell rang, Dandyosa broke cleanly from the gate and ran a very fast lap around the track. Ramon didn't need to use his whip except when he wanted Dandyosa to change leads. He slowed Dandyosa as they passed the finish line and then cantered back to greet us. He dismounted Dandyosa and handed the reins to Pedro who led the horse back to the stable. Ramon looked happy. He walked up to Chita and shook her hand. "You're quite a trainer, Chita. This horse is one of the best I have ever ridden. Dandyosa is very fast. He breaks from the gate well, and changes leads whenever I ask him to. But it is time to let him race with other horses in front of big crowds. He hasn't experienced that yet. He needs to be around other great horses. You can't give him that here." Chita did not look at Ramon when he spoke, and he noticed. "Chita, what's wrong?"

"I want him to be stronger and faster before his first race."

Ramon laughed. "Your horse is the ruler of these stables. None of the other horses would ever dare to challenge him for the lead. They are afraid of him. He needs to race against horses he has never seen. When horses race, they decide who will win. A jockey can help, but great horses are great horses. It is his time. We should ship him to the track. The sooner the better, so he can get comfortable."

Chita didn't act like a thirteen-year-old when Ramon talked with her. She acted like a grown-up. She shook Ramon's hand, thanked him, and promised to send Dandyosa to the Chicagoland track when the track opened in August. Chita shook hands with Ramon to seal the deal.

When I breathed a sigh of relief, Lola noticed and asked, "You okay, Frankie?"

"No, I've only been on this farm for half of a day, and I think I'm losing my edge."

"What do you mean?"

"I have felt warm and fuzzy inside three times in the last twelve hours. First, when I met Chita driving her Jeep; then when I met her cute, yapping pack of beagles; and now when I see her make an adult decision right in front of my eyes. What's going on here? I'm supposed to be alert and coldhearted enough to kill without feeling. Everything is nice here. I'm like a fish out of water."

Lola paused before she said, "I've been thinking the same thing. I find it very hard to take this assignment seriously. I like everybody I meet here. I'm looking for trouble, and I'm not finding it. This is very frustrating!"

JULY 27, 2006/11:00 A.M.
REALITY COMES TO EDENSGATE

THE NEXT DAY, AFTER the morning routine, we got a call from the front gate that we had a visitor. Lola stayed with Chita while I went to meet Detective Mike Phillips who drove up from Chicago with the video clip that was taken off the cell phone. Since Detective Phillips's name wasn't on the visitor list, he had to wait outside the gate. The gate patrol of McDonald and Brown never broke security protocol.

Mike was a patient man, but as he waited outside the gate, his Brooks Brothers suit seemed a little out of place on the farm. When I got to the gate, I had to go outside the gate to meet Mike. As I walked toward him, he took off his tortoise-shell-framed sunglasses so he could get a better look at me.

Immediately a look of concern crossed his face. He had never seen me in gym shorts and a t-shirt outside the police gym before. I could tell he had noticed that I was warmer and fuzzier, both inside and out. After only a couple of days, Lola and I were starting to look more like picnickers than undercover cops or private detectives. In Chicago, we were night owls and most of the time we worked when all the rats came out. On the farm, we were up at the crack of dawn and went to bed at dusk. I had a suntan and smelled of suntan lotion. Mike laughed when he shook my hand. "Frankie, what gives? You look more like a lifeguard than a bodyguard. I almost didn't recognize you."

"This isn't Chicago, Mike."

"I know. So I got a surprise for you. I stopped at Moe's and got you and Lola a couple of pastrami and Swiss on rye from Moe's." He held up a brown paper bag that might as well have contained gold.

I grabbed the bag, opened it, and inhaled deeply. "Thanks. I've been feeling faint for lack of cholesterol. We've been eating all organic foods."

"I know. Danny showed me an article about this place. For a farm, they take security pretty seriously. I've been in war zones where the guards were friendlier. What's with those two security guards?"

I responded, "They both just got back from Iraq. Like Lola and me, they're looking for trouble and not finding it. It's kind of frustrating. They're just doing their jobs. All of us are looking for a needle in a haystack, so to speak. So, what exactly was on the video?"

Mike ventured, "Maybe Lola found the needle in the haystack when she found this phone. The State Police aren't going to release the video. We hope it's the only copy. A man shoots a horse in the head with a .357 Magnum. We're trying to figure out where it happened. It is an awful thing to see. We can't identify the man in the video because he was wearing a Mexican wrestling mask and he was dressed in black spandex. Could be anybody."

I took one look at the print Mike showed me and knew it wasn't the man who had claimed to be Johnny Rice. He had an athletic boxer's build. This guy was a beefy-looking thug who looked like what most people imagined a mob arm-breaker would look like. "Tell Danny this isn't the guy we met."

"Maybe the jockey shot the video to blackmail this guy for shooting the horse. He doesn't look like a Rhodes Scholar, so I'm guessing he's just hired muscle. We found out the dead jockey flew into Chicago from Mexico and passed through Customs legally. Somebody picked him up in a private limo, and he was supposed to ride a race the next day, but he never checked into his hotel room. Maybe somebody took a wrong turn and dropped him off in a quarry instead. The Mexican government is losing their battle with the drug lords because they control the economy."

"You got that right. Was there anything else on the phone?"

"The techies managed to download all of the numbers on the phone. It turned out the phone was owned by the dead jockey. He was a nobody that bounced around from track to track. But, somehow he must have convinced a trainer to let him ride a couple of races. He takes a maiden and a broken-down claimer and rides them both to victory at very long odds, and somebody must have lost a bundle and took a pound of flesh from him instead."

I wondered aloud, "Why would somebody go to all that trouble? Why didn't whoever kill him just dump the body in Mexico?"

"It's just a theory," said Mike. "We're guessing it was maybe a way of sending a message back to somebody in Chicago. Once the media in Chicago gets hold of this story, it will be in all the newspapers and news programs. McGoonin asked me deliver this material out here. But we haven't released anything yet. The media interviewed McGoonin at a press conference. Man, can that guy sweat. But, McGoonin did a good job of cutting through the red tape with Mexico, and the Tijuana Police helped him identify the jockey. He was from a small rural village that was dirt poor but he had a way with horses. There's not much else the Chicago Police Department can officially do to pursue this. But, somehow a copy of the list of phone numbers on the jockey's cell phone found its way into my suit pocket. So, I am hoping that Lola might want to use her Internet skills to pursue this matter further."

"I think she might. So, we're back to square one, and we have no leads on who killed Johnny Rice?"

"I'm afraid so. But since that murder happened in Chicago, and one of our own was the victim, that case is being pursued with great vigor by the Chicago Police Department. And, since the crime took place in and around a United States Post Office and their security cameras captured some interactions between the man with the gold tooth and Johnny Rice, the FBI is involved, but they don't like to share information. So, at this time, they are not sharing any images with us. But, you know Danny will let you know whatever he can."

"Well, Mike, thanks for making the trip out here and bringing us the care package from Moe's. I wish I could give you a tour of the farm, but I need at least two days' notice to get your name on the security list."

"That's about the same amount of time I spent waiting in line at Disney World for some of the rides. Maybe next time I can take the tour. Hopefully the tape will help you figure out what kind of danger you might be guarding the girl from. At least you'll have another face to watch for.

Like I said, it is pretty gruesome footage. Speaking of gruesome, keep putting on that sun block; we don't want you guys peeling." Then Mike returned to his car and drove off.

I went back to the gate and McDonald let me in because I was on the list. As I entered, he took the bag of goodies from Moe's away from me. Then Abigail Brown frisked me for anything that might have been secretly passed onto me from Mike. Just when I was starting to like McDonald and Brown, they both started to act creepy in a sort of Donny-and-Marie-like way. Abigail made an apology of sorts as she said, "I know you think our security checks are way too much, but we have a protocol."

McDonald added, "Besides, if we didn't check everybody that enters or exits, we'd have absolutely nothing to do. Lots of people want to see this farm, but they need to have a two-day-prior clearance."

I raised my hands over my head, while Abigail patted me down. I asked, "Abigail, do you two pat each other down before you pass through the gate?"

"No. The night security guards do that."

"Are you serious?"

McDonald answered. "She is." He held up the bag from Moe's. "What's in this bag?"

"That is manna from Heaven."

He opened the bag, and took everything out

of it. He took the white wrapping paper off both sandwiches. Then he said, "I never saw sandwiches like these. They smell good, but I don't recognize the meat."

"Those are pastrami and Swiss cheese sandwiches from a Jewish delicatessen in Chicago called Moe's. As Mrs. Moe says, "'It's to die for!' If you're nice, I'll let you each have one bite."

"No thanks. I'll pass. Pastrami sounds Italian. What is on the videotape?"

"Detective Phillips described what was on it. He passed it onto me because he had reason to believe it might be related to the bodyguard assignment that Lola and I were hired to do for your employer. It is on the list of things we can take back to the Lincoln Suite."

THE ONE THAT GOT AWAY

THE VIDEO WAS THE first real link Lola and I had to danger since we signed on as bodyguards. When I handed the photo of the masked wrestler to Marguerite, she just shrugged her shoulders. "What's this?"

"This is a photo of a man who killed a racehorse with a .357 Magnum. It was taken by a jockey who was in the stable at the same time. Despite his bulk, the man wearing the Lucha Libre Mexican wrestling mask eluded his pursuers. The jockey slipped out of the barn and blended into the crowd. Then he flew to Chicago to ride in a race the next day. He never reported to the track. Instead, he was found dead in a quarry in Stickney. Lola recovered the jockey's cell phone and sent it to our associates in the Chicago Police Department. If Lola had not found the phone, and the police department had not retrieved the video, we would be working in the dark. Lola is very good at separating fact from fiction."

Marguerite agreed to allow Lola to examine the video. Marguerite seemed genuinely horrified by what she saw. She hoped Lola would be able to find the man. "Where did he come from?" asked Marguerite. "This is such a brutal act."

"The Mexican authorities are investigating it, and they asked us to give them some more time."

I asked Marguerite if she thought we should increase security on the farm. She said she was confident in her security crew. She told us her husband was scheduled to spend time at the farm the following week and changing security procedures might be more dangerous than going with what was in place. She confided that Clay didn't like last-minute changes because he felt too many changes often led to more mistakes.

We all went about our business. I would stay with Chita for the afternoon while she worked with her tutors. Lola took the video to the Lincoln Suite to study it.

I decided to put my time to good use by thinking through the case. The reality was the Chicago Police Department would do their best to find out who had murdered Johnny Rice, but now that the FBI was involved, they might encounter problems and delays. It made for an interesting news story, but no self-respecting, experienced killer would ever want to attract attention to a murder. The evidence we gained from the cell phone needed to be studied further. Either we got very lucky and the killer made a big mistake, or the killer wanted us to find the phone.

The incident took place in Tijuana. The cell phone provided us with the horse killer's bizarre image. There was no way to know if he was somehow connected to Edensgate. If we were going to find a link to these events, I needed to start an unauthorized investigation of the farm and its people. Something about the idyllic life on The Farm of the Future wasn't kosher, and it wasn't our pastrami sandwiches from Moe's. Whatever Lola and I were going to find, we needed to discover it on our own because evidence was not forthcoming.

JULY 27, 2006/12:00 P.M.
ALMOST PERFECT

LIFE ON THE FARM is not like life in the city. Noon is midday for people that work a nine-to-five job. On the farm, the workday started at five and noon was seven hours into the day. Traditionally, farmers worked from sunrise to sunset or until all the jobs were done. So, when I went to the main house, I knew Marguerite would be in her office managing all the financial affairs of the farm. I knocked on her door and she motioned for me to come in. "Is anything wrong?" she asked.

"Yes," I answered.

"Did something happen?"

"No. But, I need to ask you some questions." She motioned for me to sit down. "Lola and I are a bit confused. We know we have been hired to be bodyguards for your daughter, but we don't really know what we are a protecting her from."

"You were hired as a precaution. There is no specific threat that I know of."

91

"A mother's intuition?"

"I'm a cautious, controlling person by nature. I like a sense of order in my life. I'd rather err on the side of caution."

"Edensgate is evidence of that. Everywhere you look, there is perfection. And, you look to the future with the wind and bio-fuel production. At a time when many people are struggling, you have created jobs."

"I hope to create more."

"Since we were hired by you, some unpleasant things have come to our attention. A Chicago undercover officer was murdered."

"What has that got to do with this?"

"Lola and I are a private investigation team. We work for elite clientele and we are available by referral only. Our services are not available to the public. That is why we work on a strictly cash basis. There are no records of anything we do."

"I know. That is why I hired you."

"We picked up our assignment from a United States Post Office box. Only we knew which box it was in and which day it would arrive."

"How dramatic. You make a simple job of being hired as a bodyguard sound like espionage."

"I'm afraid something much bigger is at stake here. An undercover police detective who was supposed to hand off our assignment to us was killed the night before we went to pick it up, but a man impersonating him led us to another homicide. A jockey from Tijuana was found float-ing in a lake at the bottom of a rock quarry. This is a thoroughbred horse farm. You hired us to do a job, so we are doing what you asked. We don't take our work lightly. You would have never hired us unless you suspected your daughter might be in danger. We are not the police; we are private investigators that work for you. I thought this was something you should know about."

Marguerite looked genuinely shocked. "Why did he kill a thoroughbred racehorse?"

"We don't know. The little evidence we have is in a safe place. We think both incidents might be related. An undercover police officer was killed while handing off our assignment to you, and his killer impersonated him and led us to the stone quarry. So obviously there is a connection to Edensgate, and there is a potential threat to your daughter, whether you like it or not. This may be well beyond your control, so we'll keep close tabs on Chita. I would also alert your husband. He may be able to shed some light on the situation. Is there anything you'd like to share with me?"

"I guess I got more than I bargained for when I hired you and Lola. Maybe I haven't been as much in control of the situation as I thought I was. Before I hired you, we already had an exceptional security team and systems in place for Edensgate. I was looking to you to provide security for Chita while she is in Chicago. I consulted my husband,

and he thought hiring you was a good idea. Clay is a very powerful man. He spends most of his time traveling between the Middle East, his company in Texas, and the Gulf of Mexico where the oil is. Chita is my responsibility. When Clay arrives later this week, you can ask him yourself. Since it involves the safety of his daughter, I'm sure he will tell you. I sent him an e-mail, and he approved of what I did."

As I ended my conversation with Marguerite, I wasn't sure everything was under control.

JULY 27, 2006/12:20 P.M.
HORSE POWER MEETS HORSEPOWER

AFTER TALKING WITH MARGUERITE, I drove the Olds to the stables to see what Chita and Lola were up to. My arrival was greeted by the excited baying of Joe, Shirley, and Mary. Sheriff sat in the shade of a spreading chestnut tree keeping the peace. Chita, Lola, and a groom were laughing and spraying water at each other. They were supposedly giving Dandyosa a bath, but it looked like they were having a good time to me.

As I approached them, I called out, "Mind if I drive the Olds back here so I can wash and wax it?"

Lola waved and said, "Sure, drive it over and get in line."

The minute I put the Olds in park, Lola, Chita, and the groom all turned their hoses on me. Dandyosa watched what was happening. He shook himself to get all the water off and nodded his head in approval.

95

Chita told the groom to get the next horse ready for a bath.

"Well, since you soaked me down, I might as well wash the road grime off the Olds."

Dandyosa nodded his head and snorted.

"I thought it was a great opportunity to let horsepower meet horse power!"

Dandyosa walked toward me like John Wayne and shook all the remaining water on me. "Dandyosa has a great sense of humor—for a horse!" I said.

Chita said, "We call that horseplay."

After Chita finished drying off Dandyosa, she walked up to me and said, "Guess what?"

"What?"

"Lola showed me her gun this morning and let me hold it. I never held a gun before. It was heavier than I thought it would be."

Since I had just told Marguerite about a man shooting a racehorse, I didn't think Lola could have picked a worse time to let Chita hold a handgun for the first time. I was speechless, but Lola just shrugged her shoulders and grinned. "She lives on a farm in the middle of nowhere. When I was her age, my grandmother gave me a .22 rifle for my birthday."

Then Chita said, "Lola is going to teach me how to use her handgun. We're going to shoot beer cans." She asked Lola, "What are beer cans, anyway? Should I ask my mom if we have any?"

"No, you better not. I'm positive she doesn't have any empty ones lying around. We'll find something else to shoot at. Why don't you finish up with Dandyosa while I talk with Frankie." Chita walked away and Dandyosa followed her. Once she was out of earshot, Lola asked, "What's up, Frankie?"

"Don't you think you should ask her mother before you let her shoot your .38?"

"What do you think her mother would say?"

"I think she would say no."

"I agree. But, just for argument's sake, what do you think her father would say?"

I thought about it before answering. "I think he would say yes. He's from Texas."

"See my logic?"

"Strangely, I do."

"What's in the folder?"

"The files of the man who shot the horse. I got Marguerite to install a computer with Internet access into our room. I figured you could get some investigative work done. So, how about if we put off the target practice? We're here to protect her, not teach her how to protect herself."

Lola was disappointed about postponing target practice because firing a weapon was always a good way for her to get rid of pent-up anger. But, she knew we had a job to do, and once she got Internet access, she'd put all her energies into finding the man who killed the horse.

We helped Chita finish grooming Dandyosa. Then Chita dropped Lola at the Lincoln Suite so she could begin her work. Since Lola was going to be busy, Chita offered to take me on a tour of the farm in her Jeep. Since I hadn't seen the entire farm yet, I took her up on the offer.

Just north of the stables and the track were endless fields of corn. We drove west for miles along a sea of green. Corn was the major crop on the farm, but Chita also showed me the family fruit and vegetable gardens. They were on the western edge of the cornfields. There were lots of staples like tomatoes, green beans, lettuce, onions, potatoes, squash, and herbs. There were lots of fruits, too, like strawberries, raspberries, blackberries, and blueberries. Automatic sprinkler systems watered all the crops. There were orchards, too, with cherry, pear, peach, and apple trees.

Then we drove to the northern edge of the farm and turned east. On the east side of the farm was an industrial area that included a power distribution center for all the windmills, a grist mill where they processed corn, and a small ethanol plant. There were also several service buildings for the equipment and a maintenance garage to fix whatever needed to be repaired.

It was a self-sufficient facility. Separated from the industrial part of the farm, on the northeast side, was a small forest. I thought that might be a good place for Chita to learn to shoot Lola's

.38, but I didn't really want that to happen. Then, I spotted a path that went into the forest, and I asked Chita what it led to. Rather than tell me, she parked the Jeep and decided to show me. We walked about a half mile into the woods on a path that was beginning to become overgrown. On the very edge of the farm was a moderately large building that seemed to have been shut down for awhile. If you didn't know it was there, you would not guess that it would be there. I asked Chita what it was used for.

"This was the first building Mom built on the farm. It was built by the man who designed the farm. He was a professor my mom had in college. She always told me he was a genius."

"Why did she hire him?" I asked.

"In the classes she took with him, he always talked about The Farm of the Future. He had some new ideas about farming. His name was Dr. Fahlgren. I was little, so I don't remember much about him. But, that was where he lived while he designed and supervised the construction of the farm."

"Where did he go after he built the farm?"

"I'm not sure. When he finished the job, his work was done so he just sort of disappeared. We haven't seen him since. But, I'm pretty sure he's teaching somewhere. When I go to college, maybe I can study with him too."

Next Chita drove me south along the eastern

border of the farm. Along the way Chita pointed out two man-made lakes. One was stocked with trout, and the other was stocked with largemouth bass, Illinois' favorite game fish. Since the farm was fenced, there were no deer problems. There are large numbers of whitetail deer in the state, and they can become a nuisance; so deer hunting is a favorite Illinois pastime. If a driver is willing to pay extra, they can buy custom Illinois license plates with either bass or deer on them to let all who see the plates know the driver is a gamesman. (In most cases, a hunting rifle in the rear window of a pickup truck is enough to make the same statement.)

After we passed the lakes, we turned west when we reached the southern border of the farm. East of the entrance gate, there was housing for all of the workers. The housing was first-class, and the workers got free heat, electricity, and all the produce, bass, and trout they could eat. They had a soccer field and a baseball field. It was a very Pullmanesque type of facility. George Pullman was a visionary industrialist of Illinois, like Marguerite. He built a town for his workers. He made his fortune building Pullman Passenger Cars for many of the railroads in the United States beginning around the turn of the twentieth century. These days all that was left of his idyllic workers' community was a museum in Pullman, Illinois.

Edensgate seemed to run like a well-oiled

machine, and the workers seemed to be content. When I recalled sleeping in the house of the evicted family earlier in the week, I realized they would have been much better off living and working on this farm than they were living in Chicago, even if they got their house back, because there was no unemployment at Edensgate Farm.

Life on the farm was good; the families were happy and financially stable. Back in Chicago, families were having trouble making ends meet, and the crime rate rose like the temperature during the summer. However, that's not to say there weren't disagreements among the workers from time to time. When people live in close quarters, there are always disagreements and malcontents.

I figured it might be a good idea to ask Chita if my impression of the workers' happy lifestyle was accurate. She told me they were. By and large there were very few problems. It was a community that worked together and played together. Chita told me that on Saturday nights, the workers liked to go into town to have some fun. Pleasant Ridge still had a Grange Hall, a small movie theatre, and their shopping palace was the Dollar General. The farm's bus took the workers into town and then brought them back at night for free. On Sundays, many of them went to the multi-denominational church in town. The town was dry so there wasn't much for the local sheriff to do. It seemed like a great place to raise children.

Chita certainly was mature beyond her years. She was always learning to do new things, and she seemed well adjusted for the only kid of two very wealthy people.

It took a couple of hours to see the whole farm, and Chita dropped me off at the Lincoln Suite so she could spend some time with her tutor. Even though she was only thirteen, she had completed her junior year high school courses. When she dropped me off, Chita asked me to tell her about my car. "Until you came here, I never saw a car like yours before. What is it?"

"Not too many of them are around anymore. It is an Oldsmobile, which was one of America's first car companies. They stopped making Oldsmobiles a few years ago. So, my Oldsmobile is an orphan."

"What does that mean?"

"When a car company ceases production, the cars it made that are still running don't have a company to stand behind them anymore and people call them orphans."

"Wow! That's sort of sad."

"It is but, it's hard not to love an orphan; so they get taken care of pretty well. Since it's hard to get parts for orphans, the ones that people save are the special ones. Mine is a 442. It has over 400 horsepower."

Chita's eyebrows raised. "Wow. That's a lot of horses! Think I could drive it?"

"Well, I think you need to get a driver's license first to make it legal."

"But, you know I'm a good driver."

"I know, but that is a lot of horsepower, and you need to work your way up to it."

"Does Lola ever drive it?"

"She does. But, she has her own car. It's a Beetle."

"A what?"

"That's the nickname of a car they make in Germany. The body has a rounded shape that is sort of like a beetle's shell."

"I don't think I ever saw one."

"City people like them more than country people because they're small and easy to fit into small parking places in the city. In farm country, there are probably more Jeeps and pickup trucks."

"We got a lot of those. So, driving your car would be like four hundred Dandyosas?"

"Well, Dandyosa is probably a lot more powerful than the average horse, but my car has a lot more power than necessary."

"Then why do you have it?"

I whispered in her ear, "Sometimes, I need to chase down bad guys."

A light bulb went on in Chita's eyes, and she smiled. "Okay, I get it. That seems like a good idea. Can I drive it after I get my driver's license?"

"You bet. But, unless you're a cop, you'll have to drive the speed limit."

"Okay. Will you give me a ride sometime?'

"Sure. It's a sweet ride even if you drive under the limit. Thanks for the tour." I hopped out of the Jeep and walked toward the Lincoln Suite.

LOLA GOOGLES THE SHOOTER

WHEN I ENTERED THE Lincoln Suite, Lola was hard at work on the computer. She looked frazzled and sounded irritated and frustrated.

"Frankie, you need to be an angel to gain entrance to Edensgate. If Donny and Marie applied for a job here, they would be turned away. I've been researching background checks on farm-workers that were turned away from Edensgate because they didn't have a passport, no driver's license, and no references. Even a speeding ticket requires a disqualification for an application for employment and a six-month waiting period. But, workers are allowed to visit their relatives if they board a bus and spend time with their relatives in Pleasant Ridge. They must board the bus before dark and return to get their vehicles in the remote lot. Marguerite is very particular about the people she hires."

"I think that is a good thing."

"No one in our system remotely resembles anyone who has applied for work at Edensgate. I'm getting nowhere fast. Where were you?"

"Chita gave me a tour of the farm. I think I learned a few things too. So you found nothing out about the horse shooter?"

"Nothing."

"That's interesting. A model citizen who shoots horses."

"The reality is he doesn't appear anywhere on the Internet. Either he is the world's most boring man or, more likely, he avoids attention and works in organized crime as a strong arm man at the track and/or a mob leg man who does the occasional dirty deed."

"That's it?"

"Maybe he stole an honest stable hand's identity to gain employment at Edensgate. The only real mystery is why he wanted to gain access to this farm. If he was a strong arm/leg man for the mob, what possible interest could the mob have in Edensgate? That would be like the mob having an interest in *Rebecca of Sunnybrook Farm*."

"Sorry, I never read that book, but I'm guessing the title says it all. Those are legitimate questions. Did you find any links to the man with the gold tooth who knew so much about us?"

"I tried, but I think hunting for him on the Internet is also a dead end. It's not like he's going to have a Facebook page. Maybe we need to see if Danny's guys have made any progress on Gold Tooth."

"No matter how much I try to sort it out, not much of this makes sense. We got a dead under-cover cop, a leg man with a gold tooth, a dead jockey from Tijuana, a dead racehorse, and a no-name thug who is still at large. All those facts seem to point to illegal wagering and the mob. But, I don't see any reason the mob would have connections to this farm. If somebody from the mob set foot in this place, it would be like having a rat instead of Mickey Mouse at Disney World. None of this seems to fit.

"And another thing, I don't think it was a coincidence that we just happened to stumble across these things. It was almost like they were done purposely to distract us. We were hired to be bodyguards for a thirteen-year-old girl, and I don't sense that she is in any kind of danger at all. Do you, Lola?"

"I certainly don't. So, what do you think we should do next, Frankie?"

"I think we should go out for dinner, drink a bottle of wine, come back here, and make love to get our minds off our troubles, and then sleep on it."

"Did the police department teach you that in detective school?"

"No, I'm like Chita. I make the most of home-schooling except I've always been my own best teacher. I taught myself to improvise when I'm at an impasse."

"And since I was handy, you thought you'd make that pass at me?"

"Yes."

"That seems like a good plan to me."

JULY 29, 2006/8:30 A.M.
ONE PERSON'S GARBAGE IS
ANOTHER PERSON'S TREASURE

SOMETIMES YOU CAN'T CHASE a case. You have to wait for it to come to you. Lola and I overslept by four hours. We might have slept longer, but my cell phone rang. It was Danny. "Frankie, we got a break in the case. We think we know who the guy is that killed our undercover cop, Johnny Rice. A police artist drew a sketch, and we circulated it. A homeless man who lives in a dumpster saw the guy drop Johnny's body into another dumpster. He was sober enough to figure out somebody might pay for that information so he followed the guy. We hope to pinch him today. All it cost me is a bottle of Wild Irish Rose."

"Good work. Could you do me a favor?"

"If you want me to send Mike Phillips out with another pastrami and Swiss on rye, forget about it. I'm not running a delivery service."

"Understood. See if you can find out if the mob has any connections to Edensgate Farm."

"The mob down on the farm? Wow! That seems a stretch, but I'll check it out. Later, pal."

Lola and I showered and dressed and drove over to the stables in the Olds. I wanted to let Chita hear it rumble and roar. As soon as we were within earshot of the stables, we could hear Joe, Shirley, and Mary baying to let the world know we were coming. I was driving slowly so as not to spook the horses.

Chita was grooming Dandyosa, but she stopped and walked over to the Olds. As I turned off the engine, Dandyosa nodded his head in approval of the Olds. Lola and I got out of the car. "We've got to get a picture of Dandyosa and my Olds" I said. "We'll call it 'Horsepower and More Horse Power.'" Pedro offered to take the picture.

"Where are you two going this morning?" asked Chita.

Lola answered. "Your mom put a computer in our suite so I could do a little investigating about a man who used to work here. We also got some information from the Chicago Police Department this morning. Do you want to take a ride into Chicago with us today?"

Chita's eyes lit up like a Christmas tree. "Can I?"

"Go ask your mom."

Chita was in her Jeep in a flash. I asked Pedro

if he would take care of Dandyosa for Chita. He said he could, but he doubted Mrs. Spangler would allow Chita to go to Chicago with us. Pedro wasn't much of a talker. He turned and walked Dandyosa to his stall. I followed after him, so I could ask him more questions.

"Pedro, why do you think Marguerite wouldn't want Chita to go with us?"

"She is very protective of her daughter. I don't think Chita has ever been to Chicago. She has been to the airport for trips to Brazil, but I don't think she has actually been in the city."

"Why?"

"Chita's world is here. Her mother has a regimen and goals in place for her to achieve. It might distract her from her studies. If Chita saw Chicago, I think her mother thinks it might change her."

"She is an amazing kid, but she'll eventually need to expand her horizons."

Pedro didn't answer right away. "Mrs. Spangler doesn't make decisions quickly. Her plan was to let Chita spend time in late August at Chicagoland to prepare for the race. It is outside the city itself, and, in a way, life at a racetrack is almost like being here at the farm. Chita has a sense of purpose for that trip. It is something she feels is worth working hard for."

"Since she's paying us, I have to respect Marguerite's decision. But her daughter is one of the most levelheaded thirteen-year-olds I've ever met.

I guess lots of people never get to see Chicago and live happy, normal lives. We're just going to the police station so there wouldn't be much to see anyway. I need to have a meeting with my contact in the police department and pick up some information. She would be in a very secure location; so she would be safe."

Pedro shook his head and said, "Safety is not the issue for Marguerite. Chita has been very isolated here. The farm has been her whole world. It is a matter of parenting. I grew up in South America, and we did not stray far from home because we couldn't afford to travel. My family was my world, and I am grateful to this day that my parents raised me as they did. They made me what I am. I am a hard worker and I take pride in my job. I was a man before I ventured out of my village. Mrs. Spangler is very old-fashioned. She wants to keep Chita close as long as she can."

"Would it hurt if she saw Chicago a little early?"

"Again, let me say, that is not the way Mrs. Spangler thinks. Seeing Chicago was never in the plans. Racing Dandyosa will be a reward for Chita's hard work. If Dandyosa is as good as we all think he is, she will learn that hard work pays off."

My cell phone rang and I answered it. It was Marguerite. "Mr. Turk, I'm sorry, but I cannot allow you to take Chita to Chicago today. I understand that you need to make a trip to the police station, but Lola will have to stay here to make sure Chita is safe."

"Understood."

"Have a safe trip." And then she curtly ended the call.

I turned to Pedro and gave him the news. "You sure got that one right. I decided it wouldn't be smart to argue with her."

"That's how I keep my job. She tells me what to do, and I do it. No questions asked."

"Do you think this is good for Chita?"

"Yes. This is not a decision to be rushed."

"Any other advice?"

"Keep it under the speed limit. The county sheriff sets up radar traps."

"If everybody around here knows that, how does he ever catch anybody?"

"He's protecting us. It's the people passing through that get the tickets."

I couldn't argue with that. I broke the news to Lola that I had to make the trip myself. She took it in stride. Chita wasn't upset either. She said she could wait a few more weeks to make the trip. She said she was really excited about going, but when she thought about it, she didn't want to disrupt Dandyosa's schedule and regimen.

I put my overnight bag in the Olds and hit the road for Chicago.

GAS RISES

I TOOK PEDRO'S ADVICE and kept it under the speed limit. As I drove around a bend in the road, I spotted the county sheriff's cruiser tucked away behind a stand of trees. He had set himself up perfectly to catch speeders. A driver would not see him until it was too late. I definitely did not wave as I drove by since I still had the Arkansas salesman's plates on the Olds. That would have been tempting fate and baiting a bull at the same time. Small town sheriffs earn their money by writing speeding tickets. For them it's kind of like fishing for bass—when they catch their limit, they go home. It is very tempting to speed on lightly traveled country roads, but that can be dangerous unless you are familiar with what is around every corner. Each local sheriff takes the speed limit seriously. In Chicago, the highways are more like superspeedways than public roads. For whatever reason, the only people who observe the speed

114

limit use the right lane, and all the other lanes are a free-for-all like the Autobahn in Germany.

I hadn't driven the Olds much since we arrived on the farm, so I stopped at a gas station just before I got on the interstate. Something must have happened in Iraq the day before, or the oil companies wanted to record a record profit for yet another consecutive quarter, because gas prices had spiked higher again. Since the beginning of the summer, regular gasoline was up nearly eighty cents a gallon. The 442 needed premium, so it was even more. My fill-up was over fifty dollars. The Olds is a sweet ride, but it only gets about fifteen miles per gallon, even if I drive it like an old man and obey every speed limit. It made me realize what a good deal the workers on the farm got. Maybe there was a future for ethanol.

Once I was on the interstate, I tried to find a sports channel on the radio so I could hear what the White Sox had been up to. It was July, and they were still hanging in there. They had won the World Series in 2005—the first time in ninety-seven years. It looked like the other Chicago baseball team would be the first and only baseball team ever to go more than one hundred consecutive years without winning a World Series Championship. Some say a curse was put on the Cubs years ago and they won't win a World Series until the curse is removed. Personally, I don't watch the North Siders play unless they're playing the White Sox. But, given my druthers, I like watching Lola play shortstop, and I felt bad that she was going to miss the rest of the Police League softball season because we were down on the farm. But work came first.

Since Chita showed a lot of maturity when she put Dandyosa's training first over a field trip to Chicago, I decided to show some self-restraint myself and drive to Chicago at the speed limit. All in all, I did pretty well, but once I was on familiar ground close to Chicago, I kept up with the traffic flow—which was fifteen miles an hour over the limit.

NEW SOUTHSIDE HITMAN
FOR THE SOX?

I PARKED MY OLDS inside the police garage so they could remove the Arkansas plates and put them back on the incarcerated salesman's car. I asked the mechanics if they would put on a set of Illinois plates with a jumping largemouth bass on them so I could look like a local in farm country. They said those weren't common in Chicago and they put on my real Illinois plates for a change.

When I walked into Danny's office, he wasted no time at getting down to business. He handed me a photo and said, "Is this the guy who claimed to be Johnny Rice?"

I looked at the picture and replied, "That's the guy with the gold tooth, alright. Good work! No, hello?"

"No time for formalities."

"How did you find him so fast?"

"He killed an undercover cop. That always

117

motivates us to cut through the red tape. Too bad we found him a day late. It was easy to apprehend him since he was still in bed when we found him."

"Where did you find him?"

"In a flophouse hotel. It was a real dump. The lobby looked like the set of a zombie movie; it was filled with dirty people with vacant stares who were wandering about aimlessly. The officers who answered the call said the manager built a cage around the front desk for safety reasons. The manager asked for a search warrant, but they convinced him it would be easier to give them a key than having them kick in the door. They went up to the room, but they didn't need a key because somebody already kicked in the door for them. They found the guy dead, in bed. Somebody beat his brains out with a baseball bat."

Danny handed me a second picture of the man. I instantly knew it was going to be hard to rent the room until the manager scraped the brains off the wall. I studied the gruesome picture closely and then handed it back to Danny. "What kind of bat was it?"

"I don't know. Why?"

"The Sox haven't been hitting lately. Maybe a change of lumber might help."

"You might be right. The south side hit men are starting their summer swoon. On that note, how about if I take you to lunch, and we catch up?"

FRANKIE AND DANNY COP A LUNCH

SINCE DETECTIVE PHILLIPS HAD brought Lola and me carryout from Moe's earlier in the week, Danny and I opted to go to Amato's Bakery. It is old-school good, and every day at lunchtime the place is surrounded by cop cars. Amato's makes bakery pizza, which is made early in the morning, and you buy it cold. They'll heat a slice up if you want, but its bakery pizza, which is a little different than regular pizza. They bake it in big sheet pans and slice it up into squares. The crust is thick, and they make many different varieties daily. But that's just the entrée. It's an Italian bakery, so they got lots of cookies, *cannoli*, and fancy crème cakes. And in July, it is mandatory to buy an Italian lemonade with your lunch. It is not lemonade that you drink. It's more like soft-frozen lemonade in a paper cup that you eat with a spoon, but it's not ice cream or gelato, which is creamier. It is ice, fruit, and sugar. In case you're thinking it is sorbet,

119

it isn't. It's Italian lemonade. They scoop it out of a bucket like ice cream and put it in a paper cone or cup. When you first bite into it, it's so cold it feels like you got punched in the nose. It's a deliciously good kind of pain, though. You can lick it or eat it with a spoon. If you don't like lemon, they make it in strawberry, cantaloupe, peach, honey dew, mango, or whatever fruit they got at the wholesale produce market that day. Amato's is in the center of the produce district, and all the wholesalers eat lunch at Amato's Bakery, too, so they make sure Amato's gets the best fruit.

Since Amato's is a bakery, there is nowhere to sit indoors. Most of the cops who eat there drive off with their goodies and park in an illegal parking spot, and that is exactly what Danny and I did. We ate in his unmarked Ford Crown Vic Interceptor. When I say it is unmarked, I mean it doesn't have squad-car markings on it. You can always tell a detective car by the floodlight on the driver's side where the rearview mirror should be. Detective Crown Vics come in white or black. They have big, thirsty engines, but the taxpayers buy the gas so the brass who have them drive them like hot rods. They're a real kick to drive, with lots of horses under the hood. After we small-talked, ate, and finished off our Italian lemonades, Danny and I talked business.

Danny started. "How's life down on the farm?"

"Farmers work from the crack of dawn until

the set of sun. They eat healthy food. None of them wear sunscreen, and nobody worries about getting skin cancer. Because everybody is working all the time, nobody has time to spend money. Everybody goes to bed dead tired and sleeps sound. There are no teen gangs. Speaking of gangs, do we know who killed the leg man with the gold tooth? Or do you think this guy was a leg man for the mob?"

"For a change, we don't think the mob is related to this at all. Gold Tooth didn't show up in any of our searches. It turned out he was a ballpark vendor who lost his job a couple of weeks ago. He was desperate and living out of his Astro van, which was almost out of gas. So he thought he could make an easy buck."

I nodded my head. "That makes sense. He knew sports and he was a talker."

"Not anymore."

"What about the guy that killed him? Any leads?"

"Remember how I said it was a real flophouse? We figured it didn't have security cameras, but it did. And we got shots of the guy in a hallway."

"When can I expect to see them?"

"My guess is if you start driving now, you'll miss the pinch. So take off, I'll send them to Lola over the Internet so she'll see them before you do."

"Okay. Thanks for the lunch.

JULY 29, 2006/12:52 P.M.
ROADTRIP

AMATO'S WAS JUST A couple blocks off the Ike (that's the nickname Chicagoans gave the Eisenhower Expressway), so I figured Danny picked Amato's as much for the food as for the proximity to the on ramp for the Ike. Each day there was a small window of time after lunch and before rush hour when the eternal traffic jam that took place at the pinch wasn't too bad. I knew if I timed it just right, I'd probably save myself a half hour of time sitting in bumper-to-bumper traffic. It was a beautiful day, without a cloud in the sky, and I was looking forward to the drive. But, the best-laid plans of mice and men often go astray.

I got past the pinch in record time. Instead of listening to the radio, I decided to listen to some music. My 442 had an eight-track in it from back in the day, but I had replaced it with an iPod I could plug into the upgraded sound system. I put in some cruising music and went cruising. As I left

Chicago, I put on my sunglasses since I was driving west into the bright sunshine. I set the cruise
control at the speed limit; I was in no hurry and
decided to relax. As a detective, I am generally
alert to my surroundings and if I wasn't wearing
sunglasses, I would have noticed that the sky far
in the west was turning a little gray. The Beach
Boys were singing about cars, girls, and surfing;
so that made it feel like it was sunnier than it was.
Since I had open roads before me, I didn't think
I needed to get traffic updates, news, sports, or
weather. That was my big mistake. Weather systems can form very quickly in the Midwest in late
July. The most violent ones mostly come from the
north or the west.

My cell phone was on the seat next to me but
the battery had died somewhere west of O'Hare
Field; otherwise I would have gotten Lola's message warning me not to drive back to the farm
until the next day because a violent weather
system was forming in the west and the farm was
directly in its path. The Beach Boys and I were
going to be in trouble, but we didn't know it just
yet.

Since my sunglasses were tinted gray, I didn't
notice that the clouds forming on the horizon were
turning dark gray. About an hour and a half out
of the city, the towns get farther and farther apart.
Even on cruise control, the Olds was never meant

to be fuel efficient. But, nature called and got my attention before my gas gauge did, so I decided to make a pit stop at the Gas and Go Truck Stop in Dryden. That's when I took off my sunglasses and noticed it wasn't bright and sunny anymore.

I filled up the gas tank and used the rest room, which was sanitized for my protection. Then I bought a couple of extra-spicy Slim Jim's in the side-by-side pack with the real Wisconsin Cheddar Cheese stick of the same length, a Mellow Yellow to wash it down, and a pack of Ding-Dongs. As I paid a lady wearing a black #3 Dale Earnhardt Memorial t-shirt, she said she liked my taste in junk food and cars. Then she gave me a complementary evergreen-scented air freshener to hang on the rearview mirror as a reminder to stop at the Gas and Go the next time I was passing through Dryden. I don't make promises I don't intend to keep, but I thanked her for the air freshener and headed out to the Olds with a smile on my face. I wasn't so euphoric that I didn't notice the wind was picking up a bit.

I only had a couple more hours of driving time left. Since the Sox had a night game, I decided to keep listening to my iPod instead of the radio and enjoy my snacks with Bruce Springsteen. As I pulled out of Dryden's Gas and Go and onto the interstate, I saw that a storm was brewing a long ways off. I decided to take a chance and set the cruise control five miles an hour over the limit in the hopes of beating the storm. But, since I was heading towards it, and the storm was moving towards me, I knew I'd see raindrops sooner rather than later.

I drove a half hour before the weather commanded all of my attention. A bolt of lightning flashed across the sky and a few seconds later, the sound of thunder reached me and interrupted The Boss's concert. I turned off the iPod and turned on the radio, but it only crackled and popped. I was somewhere between Chicago and Iowa where it was hard to get a clear radio signal. I picked up my cell phone and tried to call Lola, but remembered the battery was dead, so I plugged it in to recharge it, and I tried to make the call again, but I couldn't get a clear signal.

The sky got blacker as I continued to drive west. The closest rest stop was thirty-five miles away when the first raindrop hit my windshield. Some raindrops are bigger than others and the first one to hit my windshield was a category five raindrop. I held my breath, hoping it was just a freak, but soon more huge, heavy raindrops intermittently splashed on my windshield. The wind began to whip up dust and debris from the side of the highway, and the lightning split the sky again and again and the sound of thunder came closer and closer. I put down my Ding-Dong and started to drive with both hands.

Tornados are common in the Great Plains of

Illinois in July. For some reason, they don't often touch down in Chicago like they do in the rest of the state. But in my lifetime, I had seen countless television news reports about small Illinois towns that were reduced to kindling. I started looking for shelter, of any sort. It's never a good idea to park under a tree in a potentially dangerous storm because some tornados rip ancient oak trees out of the ground by their roots and flatten cars parked beneath them. The rain was now falling in sheets so I figured I had reached the outside edge of the storm. I slowed the Olds below thirty miles an hour. The road was very slippery and gusts of wind buffeted the car from side to side. I noticed that two trucks had pulled off the highway, and I decided to do the same. I parked behind them. Eventually another truck pulled off the road and parked behind me, and then we all waited. My biggest fear was hail. I have seen cars pulverized by golf-ball-sized hail. I held my breath and hoped my Olds would survive the storm.

As good luck would have it, the worst of the storm moved to the north and passed by our roadside caravan. We all got back on the road and were on our way. After a storm like that, the sky frequently turns a sickly, grayish-mustard color. Light raindrops continued to fall for the next thirty miles. I tried to call Lola several more times, but each time the service provider said no service was available. At least the closer I got to the Iowa border, the better the radio reception was. Eventually, I found a news station on the radio and learned that a funnel cloud had touched down in numerous medium-sized towns. No mention was made of Pleasant Ridge because it was just a dot on the map. I hoped for the best and upped my speed to seventy, figuring there would be no police waiting for speeders.

PARADISE LOST

I PULLED OFF THE interstate and onto the small state highway that led to the farm. All the buildings I saw survived the storm. Crops were bent, but they would revive in a couple days. Farmers were letting their animals out of the barns, again, and life was returning to normal. I tried the phone again, but I still couldn't get through. I guessed the lines were completely down. In Chicago, it took the phone companies a couple days sometimes to restore Internet service, so I figured they would be even slower this far out in the country. But, the buildings on Edensgate Farm were built like fortresses with back-up systems for back-up systems, so I figured all would be well there.

As I approached the farm, it looked like the storm hadn't done much damage—but when I saw the front gate, I instantly knew something was very wrong. The gate was wide-open and no one stopped me. So I stopped myself and pulled out my .45. I approached the guard shack with great caution, and poked my head inside. McDonald had been shot in the head. A pool of blood covered the floor. There was no sight of Abigail Brown.

I got back in my car and drove a beeline to the house. No baying of beagles greeted me. Joe and Shirley had been shot; they lay dead on the front lawn. The front door of the house had been left open, and inside it was still as a tomb. To my relief, I didn't find any more bodies, but no one was in the house. I drove to the Lincoln Suite. It was fine but Lola was not to be found. Next I drove to the workers' complex on the east side of the farm, and that was where I started to see the first signs of life. The workers were cleaning up after the storm and Chita's Jeep was parked in front of one of the buildings. Mary, the loan surviving beagle, announced my arrival. Pedro came out of the building first and, much to my surprise, he carried a handgun.

"Pedro, what happened?"

"A man who wore a wrestling mask came and went on a killing spree."

The blood drained from my face and I went weak in the knees. "Where's Lola?"

Pedro quickly put my mind at ease. "Inside my apartment, with Marguerite and Chita. Fortunately, Lola was in the house with them when he arrived at the guard shack. Abigail Brown alerted them that the horse killer was on the grounds, and he was driving towards the main house."

I said, "I was just at the guard shack. McDonald is dead."

Pedro continued. "We know. Abigail stopped the man's car at the gate. She was wearing her flak jacket. Before she realized it was him, he shot her in the chest. The bullet stunned her and knocked the wind out of her. McDonald was in the guard shack. When he heard the shot, he came to help her, but before he could draw his weapon, the man shot him in the head. The man assumed he killed both of them, so he drove into the compound. Abigail radioed ahead to the house to alert Lola. Lola got Marguerite and Chita out the back door of the house just before he arrived. He must have taken some time to search the house, because they had enough time to make it over to my place. When Lola knocked on my door, she had a rifle and a bagful of ammo. You should be proud of her; she is hell with a rifle and a handgun. Not many guys have girlfriends like her. She eventually scared him off. Even though I have a handgun, I was afraid to shoot it. I have a license, but I'm not sure if the authorities would approve of a Brazilian getting in a gun fight in Pleasant Ridge. Besides I don't want to lose my visa or my job. Instead I tried to alert the sheriff, but we haven't been able to reach him."

Lola came out of the house. She didn't greet me with a smile, but that was understandable since she had just finished a gunfight. She just said, "I guess I earned my five hundred bucks today, Frankie."

"You sure did. Pedro told me you can still shoot. Lola, this guy must be smarter than we thought. Pedro said he couldn't rouse the town sheriff, so I'm thinking he shot the sheriff before he got here so he couldn't call for reinforcements. Any idea what he was after?"

"He seemed bent on getting at Chita and Marguerite. I guess we'll just have to see if anybody else is missing." Lola shrugged her shoulders. "When the civil defense siren went off as a storm warning, I didn't know what to think. That doesn't happen in Chicago. The workers got the farm buttoned up for the storm, so we all felt pretty safe. He picked the perfect time to catch us off guard. He must have been staying close by just waiting to find the right opportunity. And a tornado was the perfect distraction. He came straight to the house after he killed McDonald, so he probably was after Marguerite and Chita. But where he went after I started to shoot back at him is anybody's guess. I think we're going to need a lot of help to get this place secure again. Think Danny might be able to send us some hired guns?"

Marguerite and Chita came out of Pedro's apartment. Marguerite looked shaken. Chita held

Mary in her arms. She looked scared. "Did you see Joe and Shirley?" she asked.

I didn't have the heart to tell Chita what happened so I changed the subject. "It might be a good idea to get you and your mother out of here, to a safer location."

Chita started to cry. "I won't leave. I can't leave Dandyosa." Then a look of concern came over her face. "Has anyone checked Dandyosa and the stables?"

Pedro quickly sent two grooms to check.

I tried to calm her. "Dandyosa will be fine."

"I overheard my mother tell Pedro this man killed a racehorse. How do you know he won't do that again? Maybe he's after Dandyosa."

"The safety of you and your mother is what is important right now. That's what Lola and I are paid to do. This place will not be easy to secure. Lola and I need to get more help if you and your mother really want to stay here."

Marguerite spoke up. "We need to stay here. I don't care what it costs. I want to make sure we re-establish all of our security systems as soon as possible. Do whatever it takes. Hire as much help as you need."

Abigail approached us. "Look, I'm still active with a National Guard Reserve Unit that's less than an hour from here. It's an MP unit. I think they might like to help. A few of the troops just got back home and could use some extra money."

I agreed with Abigail. "That's not a bad idea. When is the next Edensgate security shift due to arrive?"

"Around sunrise."

I liked that idea. "Okay, let's all stay put, set up a perimeter, and stand guard until they arrive."

JULY 30, 2006/5:42 A.M.
DAMAGE CONTROL

I DIDN'T THINK THE shooter would mount another attack on the farm. But, then again, until last night, I didn't think Marguerite and Chita were in any real danger. Fool me once, shame on you; fool me twice, shame on me. I had no idea what we were dealing with. It was almost daylight when I felt my cell phone vibrate. I answered it quickly, hoping for some good news. "Hello?"

It was Danny. "You're up early. I heard about the storm, and I wanted to make sure you got back to the farm safely. Was there any serious damage from the storm?" Obviously the farm was so isolated and off the beaten path that news of the attack on the farm hadn't reached the media yet. I let out a deep sigh. Danny asked, "Frankie, are you okay?"

"I got back to the farm okay, but before I got here, the farm was hit by the horse killer. We've got at least three casualties."

His tone became serious. "Human or equine?"

"Human and canine. Fortunately, Lola proved to be too much for him to handle. He had her and the Spanglers pinned down, but Lola kept returning his fire until he gave up. By the time I got back here, he had disappeared. The bastard killed one of the Edensgate guards. The poor kid just got back from Iraq. He even shot two of Chita's beagles. And, since the local police department hasn't shown up, I also got a bad feeling this guy killed the only lawman in Pleasant Ridge before he attacked the farm so no one could call for outside help. Can you loan me some Taylor Street shooters?"

"Yeah."

"Great! Marguerite is willing to pick up the tab."

"I got a couple bad boys who just got suspended. Let me send them your way."

"Wake them up and tell them to pack their bags! It's almost daylight. I think we'll be okay. The National Guard was alerted, and they will be sending reinforcements to help us do a search of the farm so we can re-establish a perimeter. Can you contact the State Police and let them know what happened here?"

"Will do, Frankie. Do you have any idea what this is all about?"

"Not really. I've been asking questions, but

every time I think I'm onto something, everything changes. Send us the bad boys and tell them to bring lots of hardware."

"You got it, pal."

"Thanks."

After Danny hung up, I put my phone back in my pocket. I noticed that Marguerite had nodded off while sitting. The sun broke over the horizon to the east and the rooster crowed. At the sound, Marguerite awoke with a start and shook off the cobwebs. When she looked around and noticed Chita was gone, she instantly panicked. "Where is Chita?"

Pedro tried to calm her down. "She went to take care of Dandyosa and the other horses. It's time to go to work. She went to the stables with the grooms. You have a very responsible daughter."

Marguerite looked upset. "And you just let her go?"

"Lola went with her so she's safe."

I sat down next to Marguerite. "Lola thinks she may have wounded the shooter. When it gets a little lighter we'll look to see if there is any blood trail. What do you think he was after?"

"He must have wanted to kill us, but that seems crazy."

"He has been very methodical, so I don't think he's crazy. He waited patiently for the right moment before making his move. He killed McDonald. And if Brown had not been wearing her flak jacket, he would have killed her too. Then he killed two of Chita's beagles because they began to make too much noise. They probably saved your lives. We won't know everything he did until we can search every square inch of the farm.

"Abigail went back to the security shack to meet the guards who are scheduled to come in this morning. I talked with my contact in Chicago and he is going to send the State Police to help us. And I hired two more bodyguards. You'll have to pay them but, I figured you wouldn't mind."

"That's fine. I'll hire an army if that's what it takes to defend my home."

"If it's alright with you, I'm going to catch up with Lola and Chita. I'm not sure what they are going to find at the stables, but I'm hoping for the best."

HOT HEADS AND DOG DAYS

THE SUN SHONE BRIGHT-ORANGE as it rose. I knew the day would be a scorcher. There was not a cloud in sight. As hot as it already was, I knew the temperature would climb to over a hundred and the humidity from the storm would be off-the-charts. The crops would perk up in a matter of hours, but the people would drip with sweat and droop with exhaustion before the day was over.

By the time I caught up with Lola and Chita, they and the workers had most of the horses out of the stables. No damages or casualties were found. Dandyosa was fine Sheriff had spent the night with Dandyosa. He wagged his tail and greeted me as I got out of my Olds. Sheriff wasn't a barker like the beagles; he was a cop who knew how to be silent and observe.

The heavy rainfall from the day before made it impossible to carry out the stable's daily routine. The track was too wet; large puddles were

138

everywhere. The crew concentrated on mucking the stalls and feeding and watering the livestock. They let the sun burn away some of the water before taking the equipment out on the track to prepare the surface. Chita took charge of the cleanup; she knew what needed to be done.

I asked Pedro to take over for Chita. I was the only one who knew two of her dogs were killed, I needed to break the news to her that her two beagles were dead.

"Chita, can I talk to you in private for a minute?"

She looked haggard and upset. "I think I know what you are going to tell me. When Mary found me, I knew something was wrong. What happened?"

I felt a lump in my throat. "Joe and Shirley probably saved some lives. Their barking slowed the shooter down. He shot and killed them both."

Her eyes welled with tears and her lip trembled. "Can you take me to them?"

Lola noticed me talking with Chita and came over to us. "What's wrong?" she asked.

Chita tried not to cry. "My dogs ... the man shot them." She didn't want to cry in front of us, but when Lola hugged her, the tears flowed. There was no reason not to cry.

We all got into the Olds and I drove back to the house. When Chita got near them, she crumpled to her knees and wept. Lola and I stood by her and waited. Chita stood up and told us she wanted to go into the house to get towels to cover them. I told her I would get two of the farm hands to bury them, but she wanted to do it herself. So we waited until she came back and helped her load Joe and Shirley into the trunk of my Olds. We got a couple shovels from the garden and asked Chita where she wanted to bury them. She picked a spot in one of the pastures where the horses grazed. She wanted them to be among friends.

I had never dug a grave before. I guess there is a first time for everything. I'd been to many funerals of police officers, but never a pet funeral. I never cried at a funeral before, but I couldn't hold back the tears when Chita said good-bye to Joe and Shirley. A man shooting defenseless animals didn't seem fair. There was nothing right about what had happened. I silently hoped I could find this man and make him suffer. Chita picked some flowers and placed them on her brave little dogs' graves. She asked if she could spend a few minutes with them by herself, so we walked back to the Olds.

I hadn't been able to talk with Lola privately since the attack, so when we got into the Olds, we tried to sort out what had happened. Lola was really tough, but she looked exhausted.

"Frankie, this job sucks. I should have taken the job as head of security at the discount store in Indianapolis. Shoplifters don't carry guns."

"I'm grateful you didn't take the job. I need you. And Chita needs us." I put my hand on Lola's and squeezed it to let her know I needed her. There was nothing more to be said.

We sat in silence, waiting for Chita. We could see her kneeling at their graves, and we could see she was still crying. A few minutes later, she walked back to the car. By the time she reached us, she had stopped crying and her attitude had changed. She looked mad. The first thing she said to Lola was, "I want you to teach me how to shoot a gun. I don't ever want to feel that defenseless again. I want you to teach me everything you know. My father said it was the right of every American to bear arms. My family is vulnerable. My mother does not know how to shoot a gun. She won't learn; so it's up to me. We can't have the two of you protecting us forever. My father regularly receives death threats. I know I'm young, but if you two won't help me learn to protect myself, I'll find someone else. I don't want to live in fear."

Lola got out of the car and put her arm around Chita's shoulder. "I know this hurts right now ..."

Chita stopped Lola cold. "This will hurt every day for the rest of my life. The animals that man killed were defenseless. It was wrong. Nothing will make it right."

Lola nodded her head in agreement. "You're right. But, if you really want me to teach you what I know, you need to do it when your emotions are at an even keel. When you pull a trigger and kill someone, it can't be because of hate. Some people need to be shot. When I shoot someone, it is out of necessity. I feel nothing when I pull the trigger. You need to give yourself some time before you begin your lessons. Okay?"

Chita looked Lola directly in the eyes and said, "I know you're right. But, promise to teach me everything you know."

Lola and Chita shook hands, and Lola said, "I promise. If that's what you want, I will teach you."

Chita said, "Good. Just don't tell my mother. She would never approve. In this case, I think my father is right. I think I need to be able to defend myself."

I asked Chita, "Would you like a ride back to the house?"

"No. I need to do my work at the stables. That's where I left my Jeep. Can you drop me off there?"

I agreed to drive agreed to drive her to the stables. We rode in silence to the stables. Chita got out of the car and thanked us for everything. Working harder was the solution for everything in Chita's life. I turned the Olds and Lola and I headed back to the Lincoln Suite.

"Frankie, if you would have let me teach her how to shoot, we might have killed that guy hours ago. All I needed was one more shooter to draw some fire from him. Then I could have plugged him."

"What's done is done. You did your best. Danny called and said he's sending Dominic Lupitori and J.D. Mldy to help us."

Lola wrinkled her nose. "I never trusted Mldy because he doesn't have any vowels in his name."

"Would you rather work with Dom?"

"Actually, Frankie, I'd rather work with you."

"That's how you got into this mess."

"Oh, yeah. I guess I'll just have to make do.

"So, here is some good news. The shooters plan of attack caught us by surprise, but he couldn't hit the broadside of a barn. My plate was kind of full, with trying to keep Marguerite and Chita down and out of harm's way. He shot out a couple windows, but he didn't know what he was doing. He was just shooting at air and trying not to get shot. I waited and got a bead on where he was before I fired a single shot. I tried to draw his fire, but when he shot back, he missed by a mile. I kept count of his shots. When I finally fired back, I shot a real tight target with all my shots. Then he didn't shoot back for a long time. I thought maybe I shot him, but eventually he shot back twice more. I counted up his shots and figured he emptied his clip. Then I just waited. I think he knew he wasn't a match for me, so he retreated and took off."

"I tend to agree with you, Lola. A pro would have been better prepared. And, he would have had some help. My guess is he killed the only police protection the town had so he knew no one could come and help. All he had going for him was the element of surprise."

"Frankie, this guy was running on emotion and adrenaline. He wasn't thinking. These are desperate times, Frankie. Look at what we're doing to make a buck. Who'd of ever thunk we'd hire out as bodyguards?"

"You got a point there. As detectives, we were Chicago's finest."

"But, we needed the money."

"True, but I only took the job because I like horses," I confessed.

"When Dom and J.D. arrive, they'll track him down and shoot him into little pieces—like a birthday piñata until everything inside of him is outside of him."

"They are ultimate *pistoleros*. I wouldn't want to get those two mad at me. So, before we have those guys come here for nothing, let's check to see if maybe you got lucky and winged him."

Lola and I were dead tired, but we decided to act like bloodhounds in honor of Joe and Shirley. We walked to the site of the attack to look for traces of blood in the area. Unfortunately we didn't find any. He stopped firing because he ran out of bullets. Lola found all the shell casings, and she put them in a baggie and tucked them into her fanny pack so we could send them to Danny and get a trace on the weapon. It confirmed our suspicion that this guy was an amateur because professionals know better than to litter. In Chicago, littering is subject to a one hundred and fifty dollar fine.

The State Police arrived from Springfield around lunchtime. They stopped in Pleasant Ridge first and found the sheriff dead behind the wheel of his patrol car. My suspicions were right. The State Police would send in a couple officers to take care of the town until a permanent sheriff was in place.

They drove out to Edensgate Farm and took away McDonald's body and helped us search the property and re-boot our security systems. The farm's labor force was bigger and more skilled than the town's entire population, so they helped the town reconnect their power and Internet systems.

The shooter was nowhere to be found. Lola's marksmanship must have convinced him that Edensgate was a great place to live, but a dangerous place to visit if you aren't invited.

Slowly, but surely, life returned to normal. I knew it would never be the same for Chita. She took the shooting of Joe and Shirley very hard. It aroused feelings in her that she never felt before. When she first saw their bodies, she cried. Then she got angry. What happened was unfair. What happened was wrong. Someone needed to be punished. She did not allow herself time to deal with her grief or her loss. She would not break her regimen. She worked with her tutors after dinner so she would not fall behind in her lessons.

Lola and I knew she would not soon forget what happened. She could suppress it, but it would always be there. We both hoped Chita's desire to learn to shoot like Lola was an angry reaction—but it wasn't. She wanted Lola to begin her training as soon as possible.

SWEET DREAMS AND MIXED MESSAGES

JULY THIRTIETH WAS A hellish day. The heat and humidity tortured us. We worked like dogs from dawn until dusk. The phrase "worked like dogs" would never be the same for me. I could not remember looking forward to nightfall so much. Lola and I were exhausted and couldn't wait to fall asleep. The State Police would handle security for the night because all of the Edensgate employees needed time to recover.

Lola and I fell into the bed at the same time. We kissed, and the lights went out for both of us. I'm not sure how long I slept before I began to dream. It's funny, but I never know where I am going to be or what I am going to be doing in my dreams. Tonight, I went back to my high school days in the early 1980s. I was in my parents' living room watching the Saturday six o'clock evening news. All the years I was in grammar school and high

147

school, there was a weekend television sports reporter that kept me interested in horse racing. His name was Bruce Roberts. On the weekend sports reports he would always play a stretch run from one of the horse racetracks in Chicago on the early evening news, and he always made it sound exciting. The crowd would be screaming and the track announcer, Phil Georgeff, would say with great excitement, "Here they come, spinning out the turn!" That meant the horses had negotiated the last corner and they were sprinting down the stretch to the finish line. If the race ended in a close finish, Bruce Roberts would freeze the frame if a horse won by a nose. I imagined everyone in the United States was watching the horses racing a few miles from my house, and I couldn't imagine why the newspapers didn't give the sport of kings more television coverage, like Bruce Roberts did. He always wore sport coats with outrageous patterns that you never saw other news people wear. As a Chicago sports announcer, he even covered professional wrestling, and sometimes he would announce matches and interview wrestlers like he did the Bears, the Cubs, the Sox, and the Black-hawks. He actually tricked me into believing professional wrestling was real.

In my dream, I was transported from my parents' living room to the Chicagoland Track. It was a beautiful, late afternoon in October, and I had a great seat on the front stretch. I was reading the racing form when a pair of perfectly tanned legs sat down two seats away from me. They propped themselves up on the seatback in front of them and stretched out. The feet at the end of the legs were perfectly manicured and were adorned by a pair of turquoise flip-flops that were jeweled with sequins. I didn't want to stare, but I did anyway. After all, I was a teenage boy with normal biological urges.

A voice that was related to the legs finally spoke, awakening me from the spell that enchanted me. "So, who do you like in this one?" I didn't answer right away. The face that belonged to the legs was as tanned and outdoorsy natural as the legs. The voice was warm, sweet, and pleasant as it passed teeth that were very white in contrast to the skin that had been toasted to perfection. "I'm really confused about this one! How about you?" she said.

Because I wanted to appear worldly to the attractive voice with the great legs, I said, "I'm still thinking about it."

She sounded delighted. "So, you're just like me. You don't make a bet unless you have all the facts. I'm an accounting major at Southern Illinois."

"Well, that explains your wonderful tan then."

"Actually, it doesn't. Tanning is really bad for you." She moved a seat closer to me. "Can I tell you a secret?"

I lied to her, "Sure, I'm trustworthy."

"I know, but this isn't like a secret 'secret', it's more like a trick-of-the-trade secret. I am a professional dancer, and I work at a club called The Painted Pony. I hire a woman artist to airbrush a dye on me once a week so my tan is always perfect. I can take a shower and everything, and it doesn't fade. Can I show you something really neat?"

I hesitated, but I couldn't say no because I did want to see more. "Yes."

She instantly took off her jeweled flip-flops and showed me the bottoms of her feet. "Look! Even the bottoms of my feet are tanned exactly the same as the rest of my skin!" Then she showed me the skin between her toes. "Even the skin between my toes is tanned. That kind of detail is what makes this woman's artwork so special. Can you imagine how hard it would be to tan the skin between your toes?"

Since I was still in high school, I hadn't even thought about examining the skin between my toes, except for the time I had athlete's foot. I truly didn't know what to say, so I changed the subject. "Your flip-flops are really nice."

She seemed genuinely impressed that I had noticed her flip-flops. I think she might have even blushed, but I couldn't be sure since her skin was painted. "Why, thank you! I made them myself. I am also taking jewelry classes at the community center on Tuesday evenings, in case the accounting thing doesn't work out. You're pretty observant. I like that. So, who do you like in this next race?"

"I like Dandyosa."

"Dandyosa? That horse has never run a race. All these other horses have run races before. Why do you like Dandyosa?"

"It's a maiden race."

"Right. That means all of the horses are virgins, even the boys, because they haven't won yet."

"So, every horse in the race is a proven loser—except Dandyosa who has never lost."

It was like a lightbulb went on inside her brain, and her eyes were looking for it. "Wow! I never thought of it that way! Thank you so much! As an aspiring accountant, I thought I had figured every angle … except that one … and that one makes the most sense! What is your name?"

"Frankie."

"Well, thanks for setting me straight, Frankie." She wore cutoff jeans and reached deep into the pocket and gave me a card. "Here's my card. I'm Sienna. Please come to the club to see me dance."

I looked at her card, which had a silhouette of a girl on it. "Sienna is the perfect name for you."

"Why?"

"Well, Sienna is the name of a color that is brown, like your tan."

"Really? Wow! You are a wealth of information. I'm going to go place my bet. Can I get you anything?"

"No, I'm good." As soon as she left, I found

myself back in my parent's living room watching roller derby. Bruce Roberts was announcing the roller derby telecast that took place in the old Chicago Stadium. I couldn't believe my eyes. One of the girls skating around the rink was Sienna! When she got knocked out of the rink and over the railing, I was back at the horse racetrack and she landed in my lap.

As she landed in my lap, she said, "I placed my bet. Mind if I sit in your lap while we watch the race?"

"Why?"

"It's a good-luck thing."

The starter's bell went off and the horses broke from the starting gate. Dandyosa wasn't born when I was in high school, but he went straight to the front. Sienna started bouncing up and down in my lap, which definitely got my attention. I started to get confused not knowing where I was. As the horses came out of the far turn, it started to snow. Sienna kept urging Dandyosa on … then I heard Lola's voice, "Hey, big guy! Have I finally got your attention?"

I opened my eyes. Lola had mounted me. "I can't sleep, Frankie. It's been awhile. Would you mind?"

I smiled. "My main ambition, when I became a detective, was to help damsels in distress. And, you are my favorite damsel."

Once Lola got my attention, I forgot about the dream—but I wondered where it came from.

JULY 31, 2006/3:30 A.M.
SNOW ON
FRANKIE'S DREAMCATCHER

THE AIR CONDITIONER WAS working so hard ice formed on the grillwork. I was so cold I pulled the sheet over my head. Falling asleep twice in one night was hard for me, especially after vigorous exercise. Lola always fell asleep immediately after sex, and she snores when she is really, really relaxed. I thought about taking a video of her snoring with my cell phone—but since we were getting along better now than when we were married, I decided to pass on the opportunity.

The farm was very still at night. It was actually too quiet to sleep. Chicago makes noise all night. There's the hum of big trucks on the expressways, the screech of the El Trains' wheels grinding against the rails, the occasional burp of a police car's siren, the heated sounds of domestic disputes, an occasional gunshot, or a dog barking. All I could hear this night was the sound of our air-conditioning unit on high.

153

My dream was really weird. I had not thought about Bruce Roberts in nearly twenty years. What made me think of him tonight was anybody's guess. After all these years, his sport coat was still so loud the thought of it was keeping me awake. I had no idea where Sienna came from. As a rule, I don't like girls who are strippers. They don't have hearts of gold like they do in movies. They frequently are dumb, and life doesn't owe them anything because they are beautiful. Also, if you look too closely at them, they really aren't beautiful; it takes at least four stiff drinks to make them beautiful. Why did Sienna pop into my head? Some horses are sienna brown, but I never met a woman named Sienna. My dream girl's name is Lola, and she's a blonde. I turned and watched her snore for awhile … because she has a pretty snore.

I couldn't wait to get back to Chicago. I wondered where the shooter had disappeared to. I wondered why Dandyosa was in my dream. I wondered why it snowed. And, I wondered what roused Lola from a dead sleep and got her so hot? That wasn't like her unless something was really bothering her. Generally she makes me work to get her attention. But, I'm not complaining. I closed my eyes again and tried to dream about horses. After a few minutes, I found myself in a stable somewhere I didn't recognize, and I was stroking a champion racehorse's nose and thinking how soft it was. The horse was beautiful, but the ugly reality of his life was the fans didn't care about which horse was champion … they cared about the money they either won or lost.

Our visit to Edensgate Farm was the first time in my life when I spent this much time hanging around stables every day. The more time I spent with the horses, the better I got to know them; and I learned each one had a distinct personality. When they were all together, unsupervised, they are like a group of high school kids vying for each other's attention or trying to get each other's goat. There was a natural social order when they congregated. They nipped at each other, intentionally passed gas when they passed a horse they didn't like, and nodded their heads up and down when something funny happened. I never saw any of them drink hard liquor or beer, primarily because they had hooves instead of hands with opposable thumbs—but drugs were something else. Unfortunately people gave horses drugs … and drugs changed them. It allowed them to do things they couldn't do otherwise, and that upset the natural order. Sometimes when they exceeded their natural abilities, they got hurt. And that was always a terrible thing to witness. Dandyosa was a king. All of the other horses at the farm liked him, but he had a mind of his own, and that was a rare quality in a horse. He also had a sense of family in his relationship with the people who cared for him.

Maybe the snow in my dream represented some kind of drug. I heard that horses could be doped. But, I didn't know any of the particulars. I made a note in my dream to talk to Pedro about horses and drugs. "Horse" is another name for heroin, but I doubt a veterinarian would inject a horse with heroin. I do know cheaters sometimes dope horses with other things that either improve or slow their times. I never met one of those guys, but I do know I hated the guys who injected athletes with drugs. I had no idea why or what happens when horses were injected. I had to ask Pedro. I struggled to make a mental note to ask Pedro … I had to ask Pedro … The next thing I didn't know was … I had fallen asleep, again.

JULY 31, 2006/7:00 A.M.
I LOVE THE SMELL OF
MANURE IN THE MORNING

THE NOISE OF HELICOPTER blades beating the air
woke me. The sound was not in my dream. It
came from a real helicopter, and it sounded like
it was landing in the open area north of the Lincoln Suite. I got out of bed and peeked at it from
behind the drape to watch it land. The helicopter
had the logo of the Spangler Oil Company on it.
A tall, lean man in a blue business suit got out of
the helicopter. I'd seen pictures of Clay Spangler
in newspapers, magazines, and on television. His
hair was grayer, and he looked older and craggier
than I remembered. To his credit, he wasn't wearing a corny, white cowboy hat like our president
did to let the world know he was a Texan. Instead,
he didn't wear a hat at all. Clay Spangler had the
look of an outdoorsman with a healthy tan. When
he took off his jacket, I noted that he wore a shoulder harness with a handgun. I thought it was odd

157

that no one was there to greet him. He walked from the field to the street that led to the Mansion House by himself. Like Dandyosa, he walked with the self-assurance of a king.

Lola stirred in the bed, awakening from a deep sleep. "Frankie, what's that noise?"

"Clay Spangler's helicopter just landed."

"What are you looking at?"

"Clay Spangler is walking down the street towards his Mansion."

"Why?"

"He's a famous guy. I never saw him in person before." I continued peeking at him from behind the curtain.

Lola took notice. "Are you doing some private eyeing of our client's husband?"

I didn't answer right away. "Yeah. When was the last time he saw his wife?"

Lola sat up in bed. "I think Marguerite said he visited her in early June."

I nodded my head. "June. That's eight, nine weeks ago. If I had been apart from you that long, I wouldn't be walking to get to you, Lola. I would be running towards you like a man dying of thirst running to water."

Lola got out of bed. She was still in the altogether and walked up behind me and gave me a bare hug.

"Why didn't Marguerite greet him? She must have known he was coming."

"I don't know, Frankie. I'm hugging you, and I'm naked. How come you haven't turned around and kissed me yet?"

I didn't have to be asked twice. I turned around and kissed her. Then Lola peeked out the window and took a look at Spangler for herself.

"Does that look like a man who hasn't seen his wife in eight weeks?" I asked.

Lola frowned and said, "No." She put her arms around my neck and kissed me again. "You are a very good detective. You are also a very good student of body language."

"Yeah. And Clay Spangler's body language says he's not anxious to see his wife. I expected a brass band to greet him. Did Marguerite say anything to you about him?"

"Not really. She's pretty much no-nonsense and all business all the time. The only romantic thing I ever heard out of her was how they met at the horse auction. He bought the horse she wanted and sent it to her, so once upon a time he was romantic."

"When you're a billionaire, it's easy to be romantic."

"Are you saying money can buy happiness?"

I heard Chita's Jeep and watched her drive up to her father. He hopped into the Jeep. She gave him a kiss and a hug, and they drove off to the house.

"Well, Frankie, at least his daughter was

happy to see him. Let's keep an eye on them and see what develops."

Lola gave me another kiss. As she walked away, she said, "Wanna take a shower with me?"

Once again, Lola didn't have to ask twice.

CHANGE OF PLANS

LOLA AND I FIGURED MARGUERITE would decide when and where we would meet her husband. It took a few hours, but the call finally came. We dropped what we were doing and headed to the house. Marguerite and Clay sat at a patio table next to the pool. He still had on his suit and Marguerite wore one of her Jackie Kennedy-like dresses. The Spanglers were people who liked to dress well. They always dressed for business rather than comfort and pleasure. Lola and I usually wore Target casual, and pronounced it with a French accent as TAHR-JA. They greeted us with guarded warmth and offered us iced tea, which befitted their mood.

Clay beamed a well-practiced smile and greeted us with firm handshakes. "Chita has told me a lot about you two. Lola, I want to thank you for holding down the fort the other night. Chita said you were fearless when that man attacked."

"That was my job, sir. That is what I have been trained to do."

"And you did it quite well, I might add. So, let's cut to the chase. What the hell do you think is going on around here? I mean, this is a pretty nice place to work, and some whacko goes postal on us? I know Marguerite treats all the workers very well—I can't get a handle on what caused all this. What do you think?"

I looked at Lola, and she looked at me; so I spoke. "Well, we've been trying to figure that out ourselves. We haven't been able to put a finger on it, but we are doing everything we can to protect your wife and daughter."

"I've been in the Middle East and Mexico of late, so I've sort of gotten used to incidents like these. Drug lords rule Mexico; terrorists are commonplace in the Middle East and Europe. But, this is America. We live in the heartland, for God's sake. This sort of thing isn't supposed to happen here. Edensgate was supposed to be a place that would be safe for my family. Let me make it clear, I want to make sure that nothing like this ever happens around here again. Any thoughts on how we can get that done?"

Off the top of my head, I said, "Short of turning Edensgate into a prison, I'm not sure what we can do."

Clay Spangler didn't know how to react to my answer. He thought we'd have it all figured out for him by now. I could see the gears turning in his head, trying to figure out what my comment meant. The more I thought about it, the less sure I understood what I said.

Fortunately, Lola quickly came to my rescue. "Mr. Spangler, my partner was just trying to tell it to you like it is." Clay Spangler shook his head and exhaled a nervous laugh. Lola continued, "We are dealing with the problem as best we can. For starters, we intend to re-establish the perimeter and strengthen our security measures. It isn't as much about keeping people inside the perimeter as it is about keeping undesirable and dangerous people out.

"But, the simple reality is that this is a lot of property to keep secure. Think about it: you flew into our airspace and landed without any problem. Maybe Edensgate isn't the best place to keep your family— until we can isolate who the threat is coming from."

Clay Spangler showed his corporate presidential side, "Is money the issue?"

It was my turn to smirk and talk tough. "No. Safety is the issue. It would take an army to keep this amount of property safe. As a precaution, we did call in the National Guard. There are unlimited numbers of hiding places on a farm this size. This is a small city, not a home."

Spangler knew we were right, but he didn't like the answer so he changed the subject. "Lola, is it true you offered to teach my daughter how to use firearms?"

"Yes."

Spangler liked that answer. "Good. She needs to learn to defend herself. When I was her age, I qualified as an expert marksman with a handgun, a rifle, and a semi-automatic weapon. If I ever needed to protect myself, I felt confident I could. Thank God, I never had to use those skills, but I think they're important skills to have. We have the right to bear arms in this country."

Marguerite looked shocked and quickly put in her two cents. "Clay, she's just thirteen."

"Marguerite, she's been driving for three years. Are there more traffic accidents or gun accidents? It's just another part of her education. The earlier she learns a skill, the more proficient she will be. She's very smart. She can learn to do anything. She's already learned to train a racehorse."

Lola interrupted. "But she can't apply for a driver's license. She can only drive on the farm. A permit to carry a gun would be out of the question. I was just suggesting that she learn the basics of guns that kids who live on farms learn. I wasn't suggesting she learn what I know. I didn't learn to do what I do until I was in my twenties, when I decided to make law enforcement my career. I trained to kill people. I was motivated to do it because when I was in high school, I was beaten, raped, and shot. A girl her age should not be exposed to those kinds of things. That's why we're here to protect her. I wish none of those things happened to me. I learned to do what I do because I was motivated to protect myself. Since then, I have shot and killed three men and a woman. It is never an easy thing to do, and it is difficult to live with it afterwards. Shooting people is harder than you might think. It stays with you a long time."

I added, "We hired two additional bodyguards to help us. But, I think we should let life return to normal on the farm and move Marguerite and Chita to Chicago, where we can keep them under constant watch in a secure location until we find the man who attacked the farm. Chita will be able to move Dandyosa to the Chicagoland Track soon to prepare him for the Gold Stakes Race. That was her reward for all of the hard work she has been doing. I think the move would do her some good, and give us time to hunt down this maniac and anyone else involved. Living in Chicago for a few weeks will give Chita a change of scenery and open up some new possibilities for her."

Clay turned to Marguerite and asked, "How does this sit with you? Would you be willing to do this?"

Marguerite didn't look happy, but she agreed. Clay wanted to delay the move a week so he could remain on the farm and spend time with Chita. That made life easier for us because it gave us time to locate secure living arrangements for the Spanglers in Chicago. We needed to find a place close to the racetrack, but there was nothing upscale in that area. The safe house Lola and I lived in before we departed for Edensgate was far from fancy, but it was very secure. Since the mayor lived in the neighborhood, no one would try to mount an attack, and the secret entrance that Taylor Street created made it impossible to find. Dominic Lupitori and J.D. Mldy literally grew up in the alleys of that neighborhood and knew every nook and cranny, so I phoned Danny and asked him to get the Bridgeport house ready for the Spanglers. I figured Chita would probably want to live in Dandyosa's stable at the track, and Lola and I would probably end up living like babes in a manger, too. We would check and double check each security guard at the track to make sure no one could get to Chita.

Both Lola and I felt returning to home turf would give us an advantage if the shooter showed up. Lola and I had spent ten years working cases on the streets of Chicago. It was kind of like having the home-field advantage. But working for the city was different than working private cases. In most private cases, there was a client who foots the bill. Most of these clients are rich people who think all problems can be solved by spending enough money. That isn't necessarily true. Most crimes are solved inside the detective's head. Thinking is not an exciting activity to watch, but ultimately it is the best way to solve a crime. And no one ever knows what a successful detective is thinking. That's why Lola and I never do paperwork. If people find your paperwork, they can see what you're thinking. When a billionaire like Clay Spangler descends from the sky to solve a problem, he expects to see people scatter and solve problems instantly. When he doesn't see people running around and doing things, he thinks he isn't getting his money's worth. But, when I'm on a case, I'm always thinking. There is no discernable amount of action that happens when I think. I never share information with a client until I'm ready. I surmised that was why Clay Spangler preferred talking with Lola. She did the shooting to protect his wife and daughter. She took action and protected what was his. I got the distinct feeling he wasn't sure about me.

Once Clay Spangler hit the ground running, life on the farm changed. He made decisions quickly and he didn't bring an entourage with him like most celebrities do, although eventually his staff arrived by bus to handle the constant stream of visitors who wanted to talk with the big man himself. Once the media knew Clay was at Edensgate, reporters kept calling and arriving at the gate without appointments to try to interview him. Political candidates courted his favor, and his business advisors made constant phone calls so decisions could be made.

It was like the circus had come to Pleasant Ridge. The media arrived in force, but there were no hotels for a thirty-mile radius. The local merchants did more business in two days than they normally did in a month. Spangler's cool under fire was admirable. His ability to keep all of his affairs at the top of his mind and in order was impressive. He was like Lola and me in that he rarely let anyone know what was going on inside his head. Whenever we talked about the case, it was a calculated encounter, much like a poker game. We didn't want to show all of our cards until we had something concrete. We had suspicions, but not enough facts. I decided to keep my poker face on until I had more information.

AUGUST 1, 2006/10:35 A.M.
TRICK OR TREAT?

AS IT TURNED OUT, my information arrived the next morning. I had just finished helping Chita muck out the stalls, when I was walking back to the house and I felt my cell phone vibrate. Since the storm, my cell hadn't rung or vibrated, so it caught me by surprise. In good weather, it's hard to get a cell to ring when you're in the middle of nowhere. And after a big storm, sometimes it takes days to get the service back. It took me awhile to fish the phone out of my jeans. The screen indicated the call was from a suburban Chicago number. I didn't recognize it so I waited until it stopped ringing. Then I noticed I had fifteen missed calls from the same number over the last two days. I usually delete calls from numbers I don't recognize, but since I was hoping for information, I decided to call back. The party didn't answer until after the third ring. It turned out the call was from Mr. Halloween himself, County Coroner McGoonin. He answered the phone with a businesslike greeting, "McGoonin."

I smiled as I imagined him at his desk, sweating over paperwork. "Hi, Coroner. You just called. What's up? This is Frankie Turk."

"I've been trying to get hold of you for two days, Detective. Don't you ever check your phone?"

"There was a huge storm. It took a while to get service back. My service provider just restored the lines. Rural areas get restored last."

"I have some information about the floating jockey you might like to know."

I didn't think McGoonin was the kind of guy who would work overtime trying to solve a case that most guys would have ignored—it turned out I underestimated him. "You're still working on the case?"

"You bet I am! Since the kid was a nobody, somebody assumed a county coroner wouldn't spend time on this investigation."

"I admit I thought you were a longshot too."

"I've always been an underdog, Detective Turk. But, I'm a pretty good leg man when I sit down and use the telephone. Do me a favor and mention my name and work when you crack this case. In unincorporated areas, all I ever get are dead prostitutes in forest preserves and old people who die from living in trailers parked next to illegal toxic-waste dumps. It's not like my office is busy.

"So, I made some calls to Tijuana. I had lots of minutes left on my call package, and my high school Spanish is pretty good. I called the race-track, and they remembered this jockey. Sure enough, he rode two very long shots to victory. He rode both horses for the same barn. They were also the first two races that stable ran at that track—and they remembered the silks. But, he didn't come out of nowhere like they first thought. He was a border kid."

"What's a border kid?"

"Some Mexicans want their kids to be Americans. His mother and father lived near the border. When it was time for the mother to give birth, she crossed the border. So their kid is an American. He had a social security card and a passport, so he legally had a right to be here. The kid had four first names on his birth certificate, which is common among Hispanic people. They like to recognize their male lineage. But, when the mother got deported, she left him with his uncle, who worked as a groom at a stable."

"Four different first names?"

"It can come in handy with border kids. They sometimes create upwards of sixteen identities—and it makes it hard to track them down.

"So, the kid grew up around horses and learned how to ride?"

"The kid loved horses and started riding when he was real young. One of his uncles started working his way up the ladder at the race stables. The kid wasn't old enough to get a jockey license so the uncle got the kid a chance to ride at a couple of glue tracks in Mexico on a 'borrowed' license."

"A glue track?"

"When you can claim a thoroughbred race-horse that wins a race for $500, it's sold by the pound for dog food."

"That sounds about right, fifty cents a pound."

"Anyway, when he displayed great talent, somebody must have noticed and gave him a chance to move up in class on the two mounts in Tijuana. Since he 'borrowed' the license of a nobody, he got out of town right after the second race. The track stewards said he looked pretty young. He and his uncle flew back to Chicago right after the race. That's not unusual with the star jockeys, because they have hectic schedules. But, with a new jockey who rode two longshots, it raised some eyebrows. So, I ran his fingerprints, and that's how I found out the kid is an American citizen."

"How did this kid end up floating in a rock quarry?"

"That's what we don't know. Since he was wearing the silks he wore when he walked off the track in Tijuana, at first we assumed he was killed in Mexico and shipped back to Chicago to send someone a message. But, when I checked the flights into O'Hare, I discovered he flew first class. I called the airline and I spoke with a flight attendant who served him in first class. She remembered him instantly. He was the first jockey to ever try to pick her up and he was the only first-class passenger. She told me she is almost six feet tall in her stocking feet, but the kid was really cute and had a lot of charisma and self-confidence.

"He worked her pretty hard. He told her he was being flown back to ride a horse in a big allowance race at Arlington the next afternoon. He flashed a big wad of cash and said a limo was picking him up and taking him to his suite at the hotel near the track, if she had some downtime and needed some company. She thought he was cute, but way too short and definitely underage."

"So … what happened?"

"I called Arlington. They said he wasn't scheduled to ride a horse at the track the next day. And they never heard of the stable he rode for in Tijuana; so I checked the stable name with the thoroughbred owner's association—it doesn't exist."

"Then what happened?"

"I did some math. I knew what time his flight arrived, and I knew when I got the call about his body floating in the quarry," said McGoonin.

"And …?"

"Somebody arranged for a limousine for the two of them. Airport security cameras show a metallic-blue Barracuda with blue running lights under the frame. A plainclothes detective got out of the car and flashed his badge. He hustled the jockey into his Barracuda. The limo driver put the luggage in the trunk and sped off.

"Why was the jockey still wearing his riding clothes?"

"I don't know, but he was probably trying to send somebody a message."

"If he was a nobody, why would somebody go to the trouble of dropping him into a shallow pool at the bottom of a quarry? Why not just dump him in an alley and be done with it?"

"When I did the autopsy, I discovered he had been whipped with a riding crop all over his body. At first, I thought somebody must have lost a bundle on the two races and they dressed him in his silks to send a message to whoever put him on those horses."

"That makes sense," I said.

"That's what I thought too."

"What was the cause of his death?"

"Either he bled to death or he might have died of asphyxiation. Somebody cut off his penis and jammed it down his throat."

I felt weak in the knees the minute the coroner divulged the evidence.

"It's six of one and half a dozen of the other. In either case, it was a bad way to go. But, there's more," continued McGoonin.

"I don't think I can take any more. How can you deal with this kind of stuff every day?"

"I don't get stuff like this every day, thank God. I am a very thorough medical examiner, though. I check down to the smallest details. I also went over his silks with a fine-tooth comb."

"Why?"

"I have to bag it and tag it, just like the body. The good news is I found something else. He rode the race under the name Roberto Rolando Ricardo Raphael."

"How did he clear Customs at O'Hare?"

"Simple. Roberto Rolando Ricardo Raphael used his real passport. He legally entered the country."

I hate it when the blood drains out of my face and I go weak in the knees. I was speechless.

"I've always been an underdog, Detective Turk. Do me a favor and mention my work when you crack this case. I saw myself on television, and now that I saw myself as other people will see me; I think I'll need some help getting votes in the next election, even if I run uncontested."

"Coroner, if you run uncontested, you'll win by a landslide because I'll vote for you!"

"Thanks, Detective!"

"You have been a huge help. Keep this under your hat, though. It'll take me awhile to sort this out, but I think you just pulled a rabbit out of a hat, and I need to figure how it got in there."

"Glad to be of help," said McGoonin. "A lot of people think a county coroner is just a garbage collector, and this unincorporated area I serve is a dumping ground, but every once in awhile somebody disposes of something valuable. I take my job seriously, and I want to earn the public's trust. I was very thorough in my examination, and I stumbled over one more thing."

My heart skipped another beat. "What?"

"Well, I'm not sure what it is, but you know how when you buy a new shirt, they have a little plastic bag that contains spare buttons? I pop a lot of buttons, so I'm more aware of those bags of buttons than most people. But, anyway, his silks were new, and he pulled the little bag of buttons off the shirt and stuffed it into the back pocket of his riding pants. What I found in the little bag looked like a button, but I don't think it was. I think it might be a data chip. I'll put it someplace safe until you can come and pick it up."

"I'd appreciate that. I'll have someone come by and pick it up right away. Could you also do one more small favor for me and not mention this to anyone?"

In his best Spanish accent, McGoonin said with a flourish, "No problemo!"

WHERE THERE'S SMOKE, THERE'S BARBEQUE

HIGH NOON WAS THE perfect time for Dominic Lupitori and J.D. Mldy to arrive at Edensgate. I got a call from the guard at the front gate to come get them. When I arrived, I felt we were all going to be a lot safer. They both wore Ray-Bans, banlon shirts, blue jeans, and shoulder harnesses with handguns. Dom's new, black Dodge Charger looked as bad as they did. They silently nodded hello, got into their car, and followed my Olds back to the compound.

They were going to share the Douglas Suite, named after the man Abraham Lincoln debated. Their suite was similar to the one Lola and I shared, except it had two single beds instead of a king-sized bed like we shared. J.D. was instantly impressed by the fruit basket and said, "Now, that's class."

Dom dropped his bag on the floor, surveyed the suite, and said, "I'm unpacked. Now, what?"

"How about some lunch," I asked.

Dominic smiled and a toothpick pushed out from between his teeth. "I'm ready." We walked over to the main house, where a barbeque-style lunch was served daily. Like a great detective, he said, "Where there's smoke, there's barbeque." The servants were laying out the buffet as we arrived. We sat down under the shade of a patio umbrella. J.D. wasn't much of a talker, so Dominic got down to business. "This is lovely. But, seriously, what are we doing here, Frankie?"

"You two are precautionary measures. A man who failed to gain employment at Edensgate launched an attack on the farm. He killed a security guard, almost killed a second security guard, and eventually pinned a group of people down and kept firing at them until he ran out of ammunition. Then, he disappeared. We think we know who he is, but we don't know his whereabouts."

"And you want us to find him?"

"I'd like to see if you can locate him—but don't let him know you found him. Then I want you to attach to him like a proverbial tail-pin on a donkey. I want you to give him lots of rope and see if he leads you to someone or something."

Dominic frowned. "Someone or something?"

"We think he's working for someone. And there must be a motive that prompted his behavior.

We think he wants something—but we don't have a clue as to what it is."

"Okay. You got a picture of the guy?"

"We do. We'll give it to you after lunch, so it doesn't spoil your appetite."

The Spanglers stepped out of the house and started walking towards us. I stood up and said to Dom and J.D., "Meet the nice people who are paying us."

Marguerite extended her hand. "I am Marguerite Spangler. This is my husband, Clay, and our daughter, Chita." Everyone shook hands. "Thank you for coming to help us."

Dominic said, "Frankie was just filling us in on what happened. I think we would have been of more use to you if we were here a couple of days ago."

Clay spoke next. "Too much security can be tedious, but it's worth the bother if we are safer."

Dom responded. "Well, I haven't gotten all the details yet, but the obvious thing to do is to find the man who shot your guard. Clients usually hire J.D. and me to locate people. We are hunters. But Frankie says he wants to give this man some rope, thinking he might hang himself and give up whoever he's working for."

Clay looked surprised. "Frankie, do you think someone else is involved?"

"It's just a possibility. We're not sure why he did this. A lot of things have happened, and we don't know why they've happened. We have a lot of theories, but no real evidence. One thing happened right after another, and people keep turning up dead. That's why I want J.D. and Dom to find him and tail him. Maybe he'll lead us to something."

Marguerite said, "I think that's a great idea. I just want my family to be safe."

The truth was, I was just buying time with Dom and J.D. I really didn't have any idea what was going on. Lola and I needed some quiet time to separate out all the details of the case. There was no common thread to link the events. After we finished lunch, I gave Dom and J.D. everything we had, including the only picture of the guy wearing the Mexican wrestling mask. Knowing them as well as I did, I figured they'd have him under surveillance within the next twenty-four hours. Because the shooter seemed to be at the heart of the case, I made Dom and J.D. promise not to kill him until after I had a chance to talk to him.

INCOMING!

THE NEXT MORNING, THE sound of a helicopter awoke us for the second time in less than a week. Ramon Arroyo had flown in to see how Dandyosa was progressing. Chita met the jockey as soon as he landed and took him directly to the stables.

By the time Lola and I arrived at the stables, Ramon was already on the track riding Dandyosa, who looked great. The incidents of the past week didn't seem to affect the stallion's performance. Arroyo dismounted Dandyosa, and a groom led the big colt away. Arroyo greeted us and got directly to business with Chita. "Chita, I think it's time we move this horse to Chicago. He's chomping at the bit to run a real race. There is such a thing as over-training. Each horse only has so many races in him. It's best that Dandyosa be shipped to Chicago now."

Chita told Ramon that her parents were going to make the move to Chicago later in the week, but Ramon suggested Pedro move the horse the next day. "Chita, I know this horse is more like a pet to you than a business venture, so it's hard for me to give you business advice. But, if Dandyosa was any other horse on the farm, he would have been racing back in June. He was ready then. Trust me. It's Dandyosa's time."

Chita started to snivel, but she quickly stopped herself. She let out a long sigh of submission and said, "You're right. Pedro, can you make all the arrangements?" Pedro nodded his head. Chita excused herself, hopped in her Jeep, and drove off.

There was an awkward silence until Arroyo finally said, "Gee, I didn't mean to make her cry. It's just she acts so grown-up, I think of her as an adult. Was I too hard on her?"

Lola said, "She's tough. She'll get over it."

Ramon said, "I was also going to ask her to remove some of the ribbons from his mane and tail, but I thought that would be too much for her.

I smiled. "I think you made the right choice."

Ramon shook our hands like a small vise grip and said, "See you in Chicago next week?"

We nodded our heads in agreement. Moments later, Arroyo was on the helicopter, flying back to Chicago.

DANNY CHIPS IN

THE FIRST REAL BREAK in the case came later in the morning, when Danny called. "Frankie, we figured out what that extra button was." There was a long, pregnant pause on the other end of the line as Danny waited for me to bite. I figured it was nothing, so I waited for him to tell me. When he did, he sounded scared. "It *is* a microchip. We're not entirely sure what it contains, but it appears to be a very sophisticated chemical formula." I started to laugh, but Danny quickly stopped me. "Frankie, I need to put you on speakerphone. Across the desk from me is an FBI agent."

"Danny, is this some kind of joke?"

"I wish it were. This is Agent Thomas McMillan. He's in charge of an investigation that has been going on for the past three years. I have briefed him on who you and Lola are and that you are former police officers who are currently working as private bodyguards for Clay Spangler's family.

I also told him about the murder of undercover officer Johnny Rice, the discovery of the body of the jockey, and the attack at Edensgate Farm, and the murder of Pleasant Ridge's sheriff."

A voice that was as irritating as sandpaper spoke. "This is Agent Thomas McMillan, Mr. Turk. We've had an operative planted at Edensgate Farm for the past three years. That agent has briefed me on the fine job you've been doing protecting the Spanglers. I understand you are a private investigation team, and you have no obligation to help us, but if you are willing, I have a very unusual request. We've learned that the Spangler's daughter, Chita, is in great danger. I want you to remove her from the farm unannounced, in a covert fashion, and take her to a safe location without telling her parents."

I didn't know what to say. I was stunned. I took a moment to think and chose my words carefully. "If I understand you correctly, it sounds like you want us to kidnap her."

"I understand that could be some people's interpretation of what I am suggesting, but I guarantee you will not be charged with a crime if it ever comes to that. This seems to be the best option we have available. Not only is the girl in danger, but so are Lola and you. The man who killed the security guard was the uncle of the dead jockey. He is not the real threat. Both he and his nephew were just pawns in a much more complicated scenario.

Are you willing to remove the girl from the farm and bring her to a safe house within the city limits of Chicago?"

Danny spoke next. "Frankie, I don't know what to tell you, but you are involved in something that goes way beyond my control. I think you better get Dom and J.D. out of there too."

"It might take me awhile to round them up. They're already out hunting for the guy. Does Chita have any idea this is going on?"

"She has no idea. Don't tell her what I have shared with you."

"How are we going to get her to go quietly?"

McMillan answered, "That's your problem. I hear both you and Lola like to bend the rules. We know she likes both of you. Turn on the charm. Tempt her. Here's an idea: Have Lola tell her she's going to teach her to shoot. That might get Chita to take an unauthorized trip."

That got me riled. "How do you know about that?"

"We're the FBI, Mr. Turk. We've been watching you since the day you arrived at the farm."

"What if we say no?"

"Then you are on your own. Personally, if you two can't get her out of there, I think the girl will be killed. You were hired to protect her. I need you to get her off the farm and take her to a safe and secure location that you can control. So, be smart and do exactly what I tell you to do. If it will make you feel better, after you have her in a safe location, you may contact her parents and tell them you felt their daughter was in imminent danger and had to move her to a safe location. Can you do that, Mr. Turk?"

"I guess I don't have much choice. This seems to be way beyond our control."

"It is. Try to stick to the plan. Keep it simple."

Danny added, "Just do it, Frankie. I can't help you. You'll need to trust Agent McMillan."

McMillan agreed, "Get out of there, now. They won't be expecting this to happen. Chances are good you'll be able to pull this off."

"Who's 'they'?"

McMillan had the last word. "It is best you don't know. Just lay low until we contact you." The phone went dead.

Sometimes, it is best not to think. It is better to do what you're told to do. I found Lola and told her what we needed to do. She had questions, but I didn't have answers; so we did as we were told. We threw everything into the Olds and found Chita. We told her that to keep her father happy, we were going to have some fun and take her somewhere we could teach her to shoot. We told Chita we didn't want to ask for her mother's permission first because we all knew she would say no. To get her off the grounds without her mother being told, she would have to hide in the trunk until we were out of the compound.

Fortunately, our plan worked. No one would miss us until lunchtime. We had two full hours to get as far away from the farm as possible. I left a two-word message on Dominic's cell phone: "Call Danny."

I drove for half an hour before we let Chita out of the trunk and put her in the backseat. Then Lola did the driving and I did the talking. We had to be careful how much we shared with Chita. We told her we received an anonymous call that someone was coming back to the farm to do more shooting, and her mother and father wanted us to hide her until it was safe. She looked confused and started to cry. I tried to settle her down by telling her Dom and J.D. had a bead on the guy. In the back of my mind, I was worried about getting spotted if somebody discovered Chita was gone. Abigail would put out an APB for our 442 as soon as she put two and two together. It's not like there are a lot of 442's out on the rural roads of Illinois these days. But then again, how many people would know what one looked like?

I tried Dominic's cell again, but it went straight to voicemail. The minutes and miles passed slowly. The closer it got to noon, the more anxious I became.

CALLING ALL CARS

AS WE APPROACHED THE land west of Chicago, I gave Danny a call. He answered on the first ring. "Frankie, where are you?"

"We're about an hour and a half from downtown Chicago."

"Good. I sent Mike Phillips in that direction to meet you. He's driving a white Dodge service van. He'll meet you at an off-ramp, and you can change vehicles. We just got a call from the farm. They know you and Lola are missing. In that 442, you'll be too easy to spot."

"Yeah, I know. That's the problem with driving a classic."

"I got more bad news, Frankie. When Dominic and J.D. went looking for the shooter, they picked up a tail soon after they left the farm. I guess I sent you the right guys for the job; they got eyes in the back of their heads."

"Danny, are you sure they weren't just using their rearview mirrors?"

"Not funny. It was a setup. J.D. saw a passenger in the car tailing them pull out a shotgun. He warned Dom. When the car tried to pass them, Dom spun their car around so the guy couldn't get a good shot. He missed them, and suddenly the tables were turned and the good guys were chasing the bad guys. When the guy with the shotgun tried to lean out the window and shoot at J.D. and Dom, J.D. shot him before he knew what hit him. The driver panicked and drove the car right into a tree, at over a hundred miles an hour."

I smiled. "How's the tree?"

"It'll live."

"Any damage to Dom's Charger?"

"Not a scratch. My big concern is how the hell did anyone know that Dom and J.D. were looking for the shooter? It wasn't like he was a trained assassin. He was obviously an amateur. When he attacked the farm, he was alone. If he was part of a bigger operation, he would have brought help. When he ran out of bullets, he turned tail and ran. How is a guy like that going to be able to hire a couple of hitmen to kill two Chicago cops? I guarantee Dom and J.D. will find the shooter and, when they do, he won't know anything about the guys who just tried to kill them. There's no way the guy who attacked the farm is the guy behind all this. Frankie, if you have any idea what this is about, I'd like to know."

I thanked Danny for sending Mike with the van, and I promised him I would tell him when and if I got any more information.

AUGUST 2, 2006/12:45 P.M.
CHITA CROSSES PATHS
WITH A CELEBRITY

THE OFF-RAMP WHERE WE exchanged vehicles with Mike was in Belvidere. They used to build Plymouths in Belvidere. Plymouth is another orphan brand of automobile, like my Oldsmobile. We told Chita we were exchanging vehicles with Mike before we pulled off the highway. We didn't want her to give us any trouble. When we met Mike, he gave us an envelope with the keys to an address that would be our safe haven. I gave Mike the keys to the Olds, and he drove off.

Before we returned to the highway, we pulled into a McDonald's drive-thru. It was a first for Chita. Pleasant Ridge was probably the last town in America not to have one. When I asked if she wanted a Happy Meal, she said she had no idea what that was. Instead she ordered a salad with milk for a chaser. I guess once you get used to eating healthy, it becomes habit forming. Lola and I were filled with angst, so we super-sized two Big Mac meals and tried to explain comfort food to Chita. She wasn't buying it. She asked if the clown was Big Mac or McDonald. When we told her he was Ronald, she wondered why they didn't name a sandwich after him. Quite frankly, we didn't know. But I'm sure I'd never be comfortable ordering a super-sized Ronald with cheese. Considering we were kidnapping Chita, she was being an awfully good sport. I guess she trusted us.

I still didn't feel like I had a handle on the case. Every time we thought we knew what was going on, the rug got pulled from under us and a new complication arose out of nowhere. In all the years Lola and I had worked together, we never got to meet an FBI agent. It happens on cable cop shows every week, but in the real world, police detectives don't cross paths with FBI agents. And no self-respecting FBI agent is going to care what hired bodyguards or private detectives think in a case that involves the FBI.

We were hired to guard Chita, so that is what we intended to do until somebody with more information could sort the whole mess out. In the real world, people die every day. Back in the day when everybody got daily newspapers delivered to their doorstep, I read the obituaries daily. Never did a day pass when someone didn't die.

I always considered that as a lesson learned. For the next few days, it was my job to make sure it wasn't Chita, Lola, or me who ended up in the obituaries.

REOPENING A FORECLOSURE

OUR SAFE HOUSE WAS in a new, swanky condominium building on South Michigan Avenue. The
Taylor Street Widows' and Orphans' Fund had
bought another impressive property, and we were
once again the recipients of someone else's mis-
fortunes. It seemed like every block of real estate
in the State of Illinois contained a property that
was foreclosed on in the summer of 2006. Whoever used to live in our new safe haven must have
been loaded at some point.

We drove into the building's private parking like we owned the place. To our surprise,
the parking lot was nearly empty, and there was
no security guard. The garage was completely
automated, so we didn't need to pass a security
checkpoint like we did at the farm. There was a
booth for a security guard, but it was empty. The
sign on the outside of the building advertised
units under a million—like that was the steal of

the century—but the building couldn't afford a security guard. Once upon a time, during Tug Collier's heyday, this piece of property would have been smack dab in the heart of illegal activities. Although, selling alcohol illegally seemed pretty tame compared to the things that were sold on the street just outside the building these days.

We got into the elevator and a soothing, female, electronic voice politely said, "Floor, please."

I responded, "Thirty-five and make it snappy."

Chita giggled.

The elevator got confused. "Let me make sure I heard you correctly. Did you say thirty-five? Please say yes or no."

I smiled. "Yes or no."

Chita giggled again. I was on a roll.

The elevator was still confused. "Sorry, I didn't get that. Please repeat your answer or manually press the button of the number of your floor."

I pressed the button, the door closed, and we were off to the thirty-fifth floor.

Our condo was on the east side of the building, which meant it had panoramic lake views and we could look down onto Soldier Field, where the Chicago Bears and the Chicago Fire played (Chicago's soccer team was named after an epic tragedy supposedly started by Mrs. O'Leary's cow kicking over a lantern in a barn). Soldier Field was originally built in a neo-classic architectural style, but the demands of modern sports teams were more than the original stadium could deliver. So, a modernist architect came up with the idea of creating a very modern shape and draping it into the neo-classic Soldier Field. The end result? Most refer to the renovation as "The Flopped Fajita." Whoever owned this condo was obviously a connoisseur of the arts and invested in paintings that went well with The Flopped Fajita. No wonder they lost their home.

We tried to make Chita comfortable in her new surroundings. It wasn't going to be easy. This move was a big change for her and she looked like a caged animal in a strange and bizarre environment as she paced from room to room trying to find something she could relate to. She eventually settled into a bedroom that had a running machine in it. Since we didn't have time to pack clothes for Chita, she didn't have anything to unpack or change into. Lola volunteered to go out and buy Chita some clothes. In the meantime, Chita borrowed a pair of Lola's gym shorts and a t-shirt. Chita closed the door behind her and ran for over an hour. I guess she was more stressed than I thought she was. Chita needed to direct her excess energy into something, and the running machine was just what the doctor ordered. She came out of the room exhausted and, like all teenagers, she was hungry.

Nature took its course, and she found the refrigerator. Danny had made sure it was filled with organic foods, but it was also filled with food Chita had never tried before, like liverwurst, which was a favorite late-night snack for Lola and me. Chita asked me if it was okay to eat in the living room so she could look out the windows at the lake while she ate. She said her mother did not allow food in the Spangler living room. I told her it was okay with me because the living room was where I ate all my meals (except I watched television when I ate instead of looking out a window).

Lola returned just as we were getting our afternoon snack. When Lola entered with shopping bags full of clothes, Chita quickly lost interest in food and Lola finished it off. Chita's wardrobe at the farm was limited and practical; so Lola had picked out some surprises for her. Chita especially liked the black Ozzie Guillén White Sox jersey with the number thirteen on the back, even though she didn't know who Ozzie Guillén was. I think she just liked the name and the design of the jersey.

If life returned to normal and the death threats stopped, I was looking forward to introducing Chita to the game of baseball, U.S. Cellular Field, and our favorite team, managed by baseball's most colorful manager, Ozzie Guillén. After Chita looked at all the clothes, her hunger returned. Instead of the organic choices in the kitchen,

Chita decided she wanted to try some things she never tasted before, like Fritos, Mellow Yellow, and Crispy Crème donuts. Some things in life we take for granted! When Chita had her first bite of a Crispy Crème, her eyes lit up with more delight than I'd ever seen before. Maybe she'd grow up to be a donut-loving cop like us.

Slowly but surely, Chita was relaxing. It took her awhile, but eventually she became captivated by the greatness and beauty of Lake Michigan, which stretched beyond the horizon. August is my favorite month in Chicago. The days are hot but the nights get cooler with each passing day. Living near the lake is a special experience. The winds begin to sweep down from the north, and the white sails of boats, great and small, begin to dot the blue water in great numbers. There is nothing better than a summer day on Lake Michigan in a sailboat. I walked up behind Chita and asked her if she'd ever gone.

"No. I've never seen anything like this. This is like seeing a whole new world."

"Do you like it?"

"I don't know. I thought living on the farm was as good as it gets. But, I love looking at the lake and watching all the fun people are having. But, I don't understand why no one is working. Everywhere I look, everyone is having fun. What did they do to deserve that?"

Lola patted her on the back. "Chita, you don't

always have to work before you can take some time to enjoy yourself."

Chita responded, "Why not? It makes no sense to me. I work very hard to accomplish things. If I do a good job, I get rewarded. What's wrong with that?"

"Nothing is wrong with working," I said. "Working is a good thing—but sometimes you need to take a break and do something you enjoy."

"I enjoy work. It makes me feel good."

"What do your parents do for fun?"

"They don't have fun."

"Why?"

Chita took a long pause. "When I was little, I remember them doing things with me, and they seemed happy. But then, something happened. They had a big argument."

"About what?" I asked.

"I'm not sure. But, after the argument, Dr. Fahlgren left the farm. My mother didn't want him to leave, but my father said he couldn't stay there anymore."

"Why not?" I asked.

"They didn't like each other."

"Who didn't like each other?"

"My father didn't like Dr. Fahlgren. He said he was a bad man. My mother said he wasn't a bad man. I didn't know who to believe or what was going on. So, Dr. Fahlgren left. The last time I saw my grandfather, he told me he still gives

Dr. Fahlgren money, but he told me not to tell my father. So, my father doesn't know about it."

"What's the money for?" I asked.

"Research. He's very smart."

"Research for what?"

Chita shook her head and shrugged her shoulders. "I have no idea."

"What's Dr. Fahlgren like?"

"I was little when he left, so I don't remember him."

Lola looked puzzled. "But, he built that building on the northeast side of the farm."

"I know, but I've never been in the building—or seen anyone in it."

"So, where is Dr. Fahlgren?" I asked.

"I don't know."

"Then, how do you know he left the farm?"

"All I remember is being afraid because my parents had a big fight and I didn't want to listen to them, so I hid in my room. My father left the next morning and didn't come back to see us for a long time. Now, I just see him a few days each year."

"How do you get along with him?" I asked.

"He says he loves me, and he treats me well. But he doesn't take much interest in me. We really don't ever do anything together anymore."

Lola asked the next question. "How do you feel about that?"

"There's not much I can do about it. He's not

around. He's always really busy, so I can't call him or visit him."

"How come?"

"My mom won't let me. And, I'm pretty busy too. I have my school work, my dogs, my chores, and training Dandyosa. I can't take time off from that. So, I really don't know how I could spend more time with Dad unless he moved back here."

Lola asked another great question. "Do you have any friends your age?"

"Not really. The kids on the farm work for my mom, so it's not easy to be friends with them. I guess my mom is my best friend. I know she loves me. I like my life."

Lola continued. "What about boys?"

Chita blushed. "You mean like … a boyfriend?"

"Yeah, like a boyfriend."

"Well, I almost had one."

"Almost?"

"Yeah, a teenage boy was hired on an as an exercise rider. He was really cute—and he liked to help me groom Dandyosa."

"And ...?"

"Well, he was nice … and he kissed me."

"So, he's your boyfriend, right?"

"No. He got another job and left the farm."

"What was his name?"

"I don't know. I know you are both detectives but don't give me the third degree about my first kiss. I only kissed him once. I haven't seen him since. So, there's nothing to worry about. I don't have a boyfriend so I can't get in trouble."

"Trouble?" Lola asked.

"Yes. I live on a stud farm. I've seen what roosters do to chickens, and what stallions do to mares." Chita blushed as she smiled at Lola and me. "I haven't been sheltered from everything."

Lola and I didn't ask Chita any more questions about her love life. We could only imagine how Clay would react if he caught a stable hand kissing his daughter.

AUGUST 3, 2006/12:45 A.M.
LOVE IS A MANY SPLENDORED THING

IT HAD BEEN A long and stressful day for Chita. When she finally turned in, she fell fast asleep. It turned out she snored louder than Lola. We were mystified by the turn of events and glad that we finally had some quiet time to sort things out. Once we were in bed, appreciating the luxury of silk sheets, Lola stared at the ceiling for a long time before she spoke. "Can this really be happening?"

"I guess so, babe. The 'Farm of the Future' is turning out to be like one of those Utah commune cults where people are seemingly clueless and far too trusting of those in charge. Chita has lived a very sheltered life. She is so smart and intuitive about some things, but she has been sheltered from the real world, which we know is filled with lots of people who aren't nice."

"Isn't that why you smile when you shoot bad guys, Frankie?"

"I admit I'm not perfect either."

"That's what first attracted me to you."

"Who was I shooting at the time?"

Lola punched me in the arm. "Nobody. The first time you smiled at me I was putting on my flak jacket in the locker room at the police station."

"I remember. You didn't smile back."

"I know. I didn't want you to think I was easy. Tough love is hard to come by."

I smiled and said, "But, it's worth it." We both thought a little bit more about Chita. "When she kissed that boy, why do you think she did it?"

"Well, a first kiss is always sort of a big thing for a girl. She told us she thought he was cute, and that she liked him. And, nature did the rest."

"The first time I flew first class was on our last case, when I flew to Maine. I didn't flirt with the flight attendant."

"Good. We're not married anymore, but I still trust you."

"Thanks." I paused and then decided to confess. "The flight attendant was a guy."

Lola pinched me so hard it left a red mark. "Lola, do you think Dr. Fahlgren exists?"

"I looked him up on the Internet. There's not much on him, but he probably does exist. He graduated from an Argentine university I never heard of. His family was from Germany. He did graduate work in the United States at three different universities, and they were all top-notch schools. I'm not sure where he graduated from, or even if he did graduate, but somewhere along the line he met Marguerite."

Lola stopped talking, but I wanted to hear more: "And … ?"

"And now he's missing. We don't know if he's alive or dead. And, more importantly, we don't know what he did to incur Clay Spangler's wrath."

I mulled the possibilities. "Do you think Fahlgren had an affair with Marguerite?"

"That would make sense. I mean, when she gets together with her husband, they never touch."

"But, in this case, *nothing* makes sense. My guess is that an affair between Marguerite and Fahlgren would make too much sense, even though it would be a powerful motive for Clay to banish him from the farm. Fahlgren did an incredible job of designing and building The Farm of the Future, so I don't think his work was the problem."

"Maybe jealousy had something to do with the banishment."

"Is that based on woman's intuition?" I asked.

"Which woman are we talking about? Me, Marguerite, or Chita?"

"I asked you a dumb question."

"Yes, you did. I hope it gives you great angst."

I stared at the ceiling to find more options. "Lola, do you think this might be about money?"

She stared at the ceiling for a long time before answering. "Yes. Clay and Marguerite are both wealthy beyond belief. And both of them are control freaks. I sense they like to one-up each other."

"That's definitely true. They both live to make money. Marguerite seems to like helping people, but I don't like Clay's attitude. Money is the be-all and end-all for him. Did you see that Spangler Oil raised the price of gasoline again? The thing that really irks me is a major portion of each American's income is deposited directly into gas pumps, and oil companies aren't satisfied unless they can report record nets for their investors each successive quarter. What is this world coming to? I feel guilty every time I fill up the Olds."

"Wow! Coming from you, that's a big deal."

"I know. I don't want to think about it, but something has got to give pretty soon or people won't be able to afford to drive anymore. America moves on gasoline. The average family spends as much on gasoline as they do on food. We need to re-evaluate our priorities. I don't know if you've noticed, but the roads are empty on the weekends. People just stay home."

"Except us. We stay in other people's homes— for free! So, be happy, Frankie. We don't pay rent so we have more money for gas. Enjoy your muscle car while you still can." Lola turned off the light, gave me a kiss, and a few more words of wisdom. "Don't let the bedbugs bite." Then, she waited a couple of seconds and pinched my butt really hard. We both went to bed happy—and slept well.

LOST IN THE CITY

CHITA'S BODY CLOCK WAS still set on farm time. As the sun was coming up over Lake Michigan, there was a soft knock on our door. Chita stood in the hall and asked, "Can I come in?"

We were decent, so we said in unison, "Yes, come on in."

Chita sheepishly entered like a lost puppy. "I heard you two talking, so I figured you were awake. I didn't think you'd be up this early." She sat on the end of the bed. She was wearing Lola's extra-large Chicago Bear's Brian Urlacher jersey. "I don't know what to do with myself. I'm kind of lost. Can you tell me what to do?"

"How about if we have some breakfast and then find something fun you'd like to do today. Okay?"

Chita forced a smile and offered to make us breakfast. She left our bedroom and went to the kitchen, where she rummaged around in the refrigerator and found a bag of organic potatoes, onions, and some eggs. It turned out that Chita could give Mrs. Moe a run for her money in the all-important potato-pancake category. Being farm fresh, Chita looked more like a blueberry muffin kind of a girl, but you never know until you know.

Lured by a wonderful smell, both of us got dressed in a hurry and headed to the kitchen where we found Chita hard at work flipping potato pancakes. She had the situation well under control, until we turned on the kitchen television to discover Chita was on the news. A serious-looking woman reporter held up Chita's photograph and said she was reported missing by her parents. They were concerned about her whereabouts. The reporter made absolutely no mention of Lola or me. Instead she interviewed FBI Agent Thomas McMillan who said a reward was being offered for information about Chita's whereabouts.

When Chita saw her picture on the television, she started to cry. "What is going on? You told me my parents knew you took me. Why is the FBI saying my parents don't know where I am? I want to call them and tell them I'm with you."

Lola tried to calm her. "Chita, that man is the FBI agent that was at the farm, and we are helping him. He asked us to take you away from the farm because he told us he feared someone was going to try to kill you. So, we got you out of there fast and brought you here. He said we could not tell your parents and he hoped it would flush out whoever is after you."

"I don't believe you!"

"Chita, calm down. Look, he gave us his card." Lola got the card out of her fanny pack and gave it to Chita.

Chita studied the card closely. "Oh, my God. That's the same name as the man on the television."

"It is the same man. Would you like to call him? His number is on the card. You can use my phone if you like."

Chita thought before she spoke. "No." Chita handed Lola the card. "I believe you. You are both really nice to me, and I don't think either of you would ever hurt me."

I patted Chita on the back. "Chita, we had to get you off the farm. The FBI said you were in great danger, and they asked us to take you to a safe place. That's why we brought you to Chicago. We have lots of places like this condominium where we can hide you until everything gets sorted out. Can you think of anyone who would want to kill you?"

"Kill me? For what? I'm a kid. All I do is study and work. Nobody knows me outside of the people on the farm. This is crazy!"

"It's not crazy. Your parents are wealthy,

famous people," I said. "They've always tried to protect you from danger. They built the farm so they could raise you in seclusion. And they did a very good job of raising you. They didn't ever allow you to be in the spotlight. You are nice and normal. But when you began to train Dandyosa, the spotlight turned on you. And that is when your mother hired us to be your bodyguards. So, she must have had a reason. You will be in the spotlight once Dandyosa is shipped to the Chicagoland Track. So we're just doing our job. Lola and I will continue to keep you safe. So, don't be scared. Keeping your daily routine got you this far. Just concentrate on preparing Dandyosa for his first big race. We'll be there to protect you. We're in Chicago, and we have a special arrangement with the police. We will be with you every moment."

Chita considered everything we said, and then she noticeably relaxed.

NEEDLE IN A HAYSTACK

AFTER WE ATE CHITA'S delicious potato pancakes, we went out on the balcony. Chita saw a telescope on the balcony and wondered what the owner spent his time looking at. I told her not to move the telescope but just look through it and then she'd find out. She did, and she was surprised. "Wow, it looks right into a woman's apartment. I wonder why?"

Lola and I smiled. I let Lola break the news to Chita. "I'm guessing a man owned this condo and he spent a lot of time looking at women with the telescope."

"Why?" Chita asked.

Lola responded, "Maybe she walked around her apartment without clothes on."

I chimed in with my two cents worth. "Some men discover that some women like to walk around their apartments naked."

"Really? That's weird. I've never done that

before. But, I have gone swimming naked on a nude beach in Rio lots of times."

Lola could not think of a good reply; so she passed the nude beach volleyball to me.

Chita looked confused. "There's nothing wrong going to a nude beach in Rio with my friends. It never occurred to me that something was wrong with that. It was just natural. All of my friends swam at the beach nude."

Lola said, "We don't have a nude beach in Chicago."

Chita frowned. "If I go to the beach nude here, would they arrest me?"

I chimed in. "Without a doubt."

Chita looked puzzled. "But it's okay for people to watch naked people through telescopes?"

"That's illegal, too, because that is an invasion of privacy."

"I even used to go to the nude beach in Rio with my grandparents. The laws against nudity must be pretty strict here. Thanks for bringing me up to date. Good to know, in case I ever got the urge to swim naked."

Lola added, "If it's any consolation, when I was on my grandmother's farm, she let me swim naked until I was thirteen, but I had to be alone."

I summarized the discussion by saying the beach in Rio was very different than Oak Street Beach in Chicago.

Chita went back to the telescope and took another peek. "Wow! You won't believe what that woman is doing in that apartment right now."

"What?"

"She's making potato pancakes!" Chita laughed. It's funny how fast kids can rebound compared to adults.

Like Chita, I was beginning to feel stir-crazy being cooped up in the condo. I decided to visit Danny at the station so he could update me on the case. When I walked into his office, he gave me a warm welcome. "Well, city boy! How did you like Green Acres and life down on the farm?"

"When I first got there, it seemed like a perfect little world, but I discovered it's not much different than life in the city. It seems a dark cloud follows me wherever I go, and the sale of body bags goes through the roof."

"Well, Mr. Doom and Gloom, I do finally have some good news for you. We know why Dom and J.D. picked up a tail when they left the farm."

"You mean, we actually know what happened for a change?"

"Indeed, we do. Both of the guys tailing them were killed when they hit the tree but it was easy to identify them after we got enough pieces and parts together."

"Who were they?"

"Turned out Dom was boppin' some lady whose ex-husband is in the mob. Dom went to high school with her, and they had unrequited yearnings for each other that simmered until they saw each other at their fifteenth high school reunion. Her ex-husband, who is very territorial, took exception to their dirty dancing and decided to put an end to it. Even though he divorced his wife, he still felt she was his because he was paying 'ali-money' to her and she should lead the life of a nun—and, her boppin' a cop didn't sit well with him. So, he personally wanted to put an end to the relationship. He had one of his goons drive him so he'd be free to do some shooting. They tailed Dom and J.D. all the way from Chicago to the farm. When they couldn't get past the entry gate at the farm, they waited. When Dom and J.D. went looking for the shooter, the angry husband and his goon followed. Needless to say, the guy was less capable with a shotgun than Dick Cheney. And the rest is self-defense and a chance meeting with a tree. So, it had nothing to do with your case."

"Good. I feared it was an inside job from someone that lived on the farm."

"But, I got more good news for you."

"My heart be still."

"Sometimes things just work out for the better. Dom and J.D. picked up the scent of the shooter right away. There aren't a lot of places to stay in farm country. When they started checking nearby motels, they discovered he was staying at a little out-of-the-way country motel, like the Bates' place in *Psycho*. It was filled with migrant Mexican field hands who had come north for the fall harvest. He tried to blend in, but Dom and J.D. spotted him right away because he was the size of a professional wrestler. Lucky for him, they found him just in time."

"Just in time? What does that mean?"

"When Dom and J.D. spotted him, he was walking into his room with a rope. Turns out he was going to hang himself."

"Because he was at the end of his rope?"

Danny ignored my wit. "The Illinois State Police arrested him for the murders of Pleasant Ridge's sheriff and Edensgate's security guard. But, in the interests of simplicity, they decided to make life easy on all of us by transporting him to Chicago for questioning. They're also releasing the body bags of the mob guys and sending them in one convenient shipment."

"Wow, less red tape and big savings for the taxpayers. What will they think of next?"

"You."

"Me?"

Danny explained. "Since we have an ongoing investigation of a murdered undercover police officer in Chicago, and you're the only one who has a big-picture perspective of city, farm, and, quarry ... and you have Spangler's daughter in your custody, it just made a lot of sense to bring the shooter to Chicago for questioning. You won't have to go back to the farm."

"Wow! That *is* convenient. I'm cautiously optimistic, Danny, but nothing makes sense in this case."

"We'll soon see! As we speak, a convoy of State Police, led by Dom and J.D., are bringing the shooter back from Pleasant Ridge and placing him in one of our empty cells."

"What about the Spanglers? Do they know the shooter has been captured?"

"They sure do. Clay Spangler is flying to Chicago in his private helicopter. I guess Marguerite has a fear of helicopters, so she made other transportation arrangements. Since Dandyosa was going to be shipped to Chicago in a few days, she decided to make the move to the Chicagoland Track a little earlier. All the arrangements were in place anyway. She asked me to tell you to let Chita know she is going to supervise the move herself."

"So, they know we didn't kidnap Chita?"

"Sure. We think of everything."

"That's good to know. Chita can breathe easy now. She is pretty lost without her daily chores, so that should make her happy. Mind if I continue to keep Dom and J.D. on Marguerite's payroll? I'll need some help at the track."

"Since it doesn't cost me or the taxpayers anything, that would be fine with me. The track will provide you some extra security personnel.

They're used to this sort of thing. Thoroughbred racing is the sport of kings, and Arab dignitaries from Dubai have an entry in the Gold Stakes Race. And, wherever Clay Spangler goes, he is followed by the press. All the publicity should draw a big crowd. So, the track had already planned on hiring extra security help."

I mused, "How you going to keep 'em down on the farm ... sounds like McMillan has everything wrapped up with this case."

"Not really. He's staying at the farm."

I frowned. "Why?"

"He got a search warrant to open up that research facility on the property, that's been closed for years. The FBI isn't saying what they're looking for."

It was my turn to share some information. "Chita gave us a little background about the facility. The man who created The Farm of The Future was an Argentine who knew Marguerite. His name is Fahlgren. Marguerite and Clay got into a big argument about him a long time ago, and Clay insisted Marguerite fire him and make him leave the farm. We don't know what the big row was all about, but the Spanglers are estranged. Marguerite funded a bio-fuel project that Clay didn't approve of. He put an end to it. That might have been the straw that broke the camel's back. Chita told us that Fahlgren is now funded by Marguerite's father."

"Wow, you are a wealth of information. I'm sure McMillan would love to know about it, so I trust you'll share it with him when the time is right?"

"Of course."

Danny looked me in the eye and said, "Cross your heart and hope to die or stick a needle in your eye?"

I hesitated at the prospect of sticking a needle in my eye, but I agreed. "Absolutely."

Danny opened his desk drawer and handed me a thick 8 x 10 envelope. "By the way, I have something for you. Here is the information our tech guys downloaded off the microchip you gave us. Nobody seems to know what any of it means."

I was stunned. "So, you actually found something? And it's that complex?"

Danny shrugged his shoulders. "I don't know how complex it is, but it's written in German, and nobody in the department can translate it. This document is over a hundred pages long. It's amazing how much information you can fit on one of those little chips." As I turned to go, Danny reminded me, "Remember you made a promise. I expect you to keep it. Next time you go past a tailor shop, buy a needle."

Chita considered everything we said, and then she noticeably relaxed.

AUGUST 3, 2006/11:30 A.M.

FRANKIE GETS A CHIP
OFF HIS SHOULDER

AS I WALKED BACK TO my Olds, I wondered where I could find a German scientist to translate the document on short notice. The Illinois Institute of Technology is Chicago's elite technical institute, but I didn't have any contacts there. I racked my brain wondering who I could call. They have a lot of brainy sorts at the University of Chicago, but again, I didn't have any contacts. I nearly flunked high school chemistry so I considered giving the document directly to Agent Thomas McMillan and let him use the resources at the FBI to find out what I had. But, would he tell me if he found something good? I was working for my client and my discovery was on her dime. Loyalty is important to me, so I was between a rock and a hard place.

Over the years, I found I did my best thinking when I did some drinking. It's amazing the answers you can dreg up from the bottom of a bottle of rye. I decided to go to the Billy Goat Tavern, the place where Chicago's shakers and movers go to drink. It was made famous by the *Saturday Night Live* sketch "Cheeseborger! Cheeseborger!" The Goat is located under Michigan Avenue across the street from the Tribune Tower. You can get a drink and a cheeseburger there pretty much any time, day or night. It is a hangout for reporters and interesting people. I didn't know where else to go to find help, so I went to The Goat.

The Goat ain't fancy; it's functional. You eat, you drink, you talk loud, and you smoke 'em if you got 'em. If you don't know somebody, you will. If you need to find somebody, ask. I ordered a Double-O-Cheese and a tumbler of rye. It wasn't quite noon, but who cared? I needed answers. The Greek grill man made my burger in a Chicago minute (which is a little longer than a New York minute). He handed it to me on a Kaiser roll wrapped in a piece of white paper. In most cases, the grill assistant tries very hard to sell you a Pepsi, but when he saw my tumbler of rye, he knew I was a lost cause. Instead he tried to sell me a bag of chips, but I declined because I don't like salt.

After I paid for my burger, I proceeded two steps forward to a counter next to the grill where there was a selection of self-serve toppings of sliced raw onions, dill pickle chips, piccalilli, mustard, and ketchup. As luck would have it, a bunch of reporters came into the place. One of them had written a story about me when I was suspended. I nodded to her as she walked by, and she stopped and shook my hand. "No hard feelings?"

I shook my head. "I did what I did. You did what you had to do."

"How are you doing?"

"I'm okay. I got a job right away. Somebody always has a need for a guy like me. Thanks to you, people know I'm a problem solver."

"I never thought they'd suspend you for doing the right thing."

"Well, I landed on my feet. I'm making more money—and I don't have to do any paperwork."

"Can I buy you a drink?"

I held up my rye. "I got one, but two would be better."

She went up to the bar and came back with her Double-O-Cheese, a Pepsi, a bag of chips, and my second rye, which she placed next to my first. "Thanks," I said.

When she opened her bag of chips, she offered me some. I shook my head no. She offered her hand as a peace offering and said, "I owe you one, Frankie. So, what are you working on?"

I took a long, meaningful, and dramatic swig of my rye and confided in her. "Funny you offered me a chip. It's even ironic. I'm working on an international espionage case involving *a micro-computer chip*, and I'm not supposed to talk about it."

She laughed and bit into her burger. She drew blood with the first bite. "Glad to see you still got a sense of humor, Frankie. Seriously, are you working on anything interesting?"

I leaned in closer to her. "Actually, I need to find a German chemist who can translate a document for me."

She laughed. "Man, you are good."

"Actually, I'm dead serious." I put the document on the table so she knew I wasn't kidding. "Could you point me in a direction? I really do need a little help."

She leafed through the document. "You're serious?"

"Yeah. And like you said, you owe me one."

"Well ... somebody at the *Trib* will know somebody. Give me your cell number. I'll see what I can do."

Within the hour, I got a call from my reporter friend. She gave me the name of a man who could translate German. He lived in a high-rise building a couple blocks away from the *Trib*. He wasn't a chemist, but he translated technical documents for big corporations so I figured he could handle it. His office was located in a building that was hopelessly lost in the 1970s, with faux-wood doors that had the same grain pattern on each one.

I knocked on his door, and he opened it. His office had fluorescent lights that made the room too bright. It gave his skin a pasty-gray tone. His eyes were bloodshot and he wore a bad wig and a cheap suit. He informed me he charged $125 an hour to translate. I guessed there wasn't much need for German translators on Michigan Avenue in Chicago, so I was stuck with him, his bad wig, and his polyester clothes.

He spoke precise English with a German accent. He was a no-nonsense guy and laid out the terms of his services. He told me he was very efficient, and he wanted to be paid in cash. I told him I was a cash-and-carry kind of guy, too, and I needed him to start translating right away. I was going to add that we were a match made in Heaven, but I wasn't sure how he'd take that, so I decided to not say it. He knew I was serious and needed the job done quickly. He sat down and started translating.

True to his word, he was efficient. He said the document was about the development of a new hybrid corn that Dr. Fahlgren developed over a six-year period. The translator related a stirring tale of incestuous cross-pollination of exotic corn silks from the Amazonian rainforest with those from the heartland of the plains of Illinois. He talked of organic infusions put into the soil at specific times of the corn's growth cycle that allowed the new hybrid to achieve faster growth. The end result was a sturdier, healthier, hybrid that was tastier and more nutritious, while creating a greater yield. The new soil additives stirred my soul because they were inexpensive to make and enriched the soil when the crops were plowed under in the fall. As he neared the end of the story, the translator started to explain complex chemical and biological details and related them to yield statistics. That is when I began to regret drinking the second rye because my eyelids became heavy and I struggled not to fall asleep while he droned on, translating Dr. Fahlgren's words. Dr. Fahlgren was a brilliant but boring man. Listening to the translator's precise monotone translation of Fahlgren's words was more powerful than some Mickey Finn's I'd been slipped. Somehow, I managed to stay awake for the entire two hours and forty-six minutes it took to go through the document.

His bill was $345.28 ($2.08 per minute for 166 minutes). Since I didn't have exact change, I gave him three hundreds and a fifty. He opened his desk drawer and gave me $4.72 in change and a receipt for my records. I told him I didn't keep records, but he gave me the receipt anyway. I shook hands with him and then I went directly back to the police department to tell Danny our miracle data chip was just a corn chip. There was no big news to help the FBI break the case wide open. We were at another dead end. Nobody in their right mind would kill to get their hands on this kind of information. I hopped into a cab and headed straight to Danny's office.

When I shared the news with Danny, he was just as disappointed as I was. He shook his head and said, "So, this is just a document about the development of a new type of corn?"

"Yeah," I answered. "I guess we shouldn't be completely disappointed. It will increase the crop yields next year, and the increase in the production of corn will lower the price for the consumer, and it will be tastier."

"Do you think it's worth sharing with the FBI?"

"I don't know. I can't imagine why McMillan would want it."

"Me neither. But, if we give it to him, it'd show him we were trying to help him out. And you can vouch for me that I gave it to him as soon as I found, and I insisted we share it with him. We might get some goodwill in return. Now, what?"

"I breathe a sigh of relief knowing I don't have to stick a needle in my eye and I can go back to the condo and wait."

"For what?"

"Dinner. In addition to training racehorses, Lola and I discovered Chita is a pretty good cook. She knows a lot about preparing very tasty Brazilian dishes."

AUGUST 3, 2006/7:00 P.M.
MONEY MATTERS ... BUT
DON'T BE LATE FOR DINNER

CHITA MADE LIME CILANTRO rice, broiled red snapper covered with coconut-mango glaze, and plantains in a bubbling brown-sugar glaze as a side dish for dinner. Chita's culinary skills went far beyond potato pancakes and blueberry muffins. The Sox game was on at 7:05 so we ate in the living room and watched it on the big plasma screen with surround sound. The White Sox were playing the Yankees, so the game was sold out. Most White Sox fans hate the Yankees. The Yankees wrecked my childhood because they almost always won, and the Sox frequently came up a little short. The Yanks had Mickey Mantle, Roger Maris, Yogi Berra, Moose Skowron, Billy Martin, Whitey Ford, Elston Howard, and fireball Ryne Duren. The reason I never liked the Yankees was they were a wealthy team. Their team-building strategy was always the same: spend the most money and buy the best players to win championships. That never sat right with me. It wasn't "sporting." Why do rich people have everything and still want more? I grew up thinking the point of sports was doing your best instead of spending the most. Anyway, I like to watch the Sox/Yankee games because when the Yankees lose, it makes me feel great. Lola shares my viewpoint, and we hoped to pass our passion along to Chita.

We knew this was going to be difficult because Chita was the daughter of two very wealthy parents who could buy anything for her. She had a million-dollar racehorse. Her father was CEO of a worldwide oil company. Her mother built The Farm of the Future and her grandfather owned a South American ethanol company. So, when we tried to explain why the White Sox were the good guys and the Yankees were the bad guys, it was a slippery slope to climb and explore with Chita.

What we discovered in the process was very interesting. It turned out Chita had no interest in money because she never needed to buy anything. If she wanted something, her parents or their staff went out and bought it for her. It didn't matter if it was a can of soda or a million-dollar racehorse. Chita got whatever she asked for, but she never had to pay for anything. Chita didn't have any money of her own, so money meant nothing to her. In Chita's world, work and success had value, but money didn't. So, trying to explain to

Chita why the Yankees spent millions of dollars to win championships was a lost cause.

Chita finally asked, "Why do people need money?"

That was the first time Lola and I had ever heard that question so we didn't quite know what to say. Lola started "How much allowance do you get a week?"

Chita looked confused. "What's an allowance?"

Lola explained. "It's a set amount of money you get each week so you can buy things you want or need."

"I don't get an allowance. I never have any money to spend. If I need something, I just ask for it. I write down how much food or supplies I need for the dogs and the horses, and I give the list to Pedro, and it gets delivered."

"What if you want something for yourself?"

"Like what?"

"Like some new clothes."

"Well, I don't get new clothes very often. It's not like I need many. I get pretty dirty working like I do."

"But, when Lola gave you the Ozzie jersey, you really liked it, right? What about stuff like that?"

"I loved it, but I didn't ask for it or buy it. You just gave it to me. It was a gift, right?"

Lola smiled and said, "Of course."

"Do you have any money of your own?" I asked.

"No. I don't really need it."

Lola looked puzzled. "But, you're really good at math. Do you know the difference between one dollar and one million dollars?"

Chita quickly answered, "Nine hundred and ninety-ninety thousand, nine hundred and ninety-nine dollars, right?"

I nodded my head yes. "What would you do with a million dollars?"

Chita replied, "Nothing. I don't have a million dollars, and I don't need to buy anything. And if I did, I don't know what I would buy."

Lola asked, "Are you happy?"

"Until all this happened, I was really happy. But now, two of my dogs are dead and I can't be with my horse or my other dogs or my family. Why did all these bad things happen?"

Lola and I didn't know what to say.

Chita continued, "Was this all about money?"

Lola answered. "We don't know why yet."

"Does my mother pay you money?"

"Yes."

"How much?"

I answered. "Five hundred a day plus expenses for each of us."

"If she paid you a million dollars, would that help you find out what is going on any faster?"

"No."

"Would it have saved my dogs?"

"No."

"Then why is money so important?"

Lola and I didn't have any answers, so we let Chita have the last word on money. Maybe her way of looking at the world was better than ours. She never thought about money. Unfortunately, she was in a minority of one.

We ended all talk of money and decided to teach Chita about the game of baseball instead. Chita had never watched a game before, so we had to explain the basic rules of the game first. Since most of each game is spent waiting for the pitcher to throw the ball, we had lots of time to tutor her. It was a great game, with lots of scoring in a seesaw battle, so it was an exciting way to explain how the rules worked.

And the Sox saved the best for last. White Sox first baseman, Paulie Konerko, hit a homerun with two on base and two out in the bottom of the ninth for a thriller of a victory. The famous White Sox exploding scoreboard shot off fireworks, and the White Sox fans sang their victory song. "No matter how much Yankee management paid their players, they returned homes losers, and Lola and I felt very good about that. The reality was that no amount of money would have helped the fate of the hanging curveball the Yankee reliever threw. It came down to a struggle between two men; and one of them won and one of them lost.

The game didn't end until nearly midnight. Chita found it exciting, and she loved Ozzie because he chewed sunflower seeds. Chita grew sunflowers in her garden and Dandyosa ate them too. When we told Chita that Ozzie Guillén was from Venezuela and was the manager of the White Sox, she became even more interested in the game. Since Chita was really smart, she picked up the rules quickly. We were turning Chita into a White Sox fan, and her introduction to America's favorite pastime was fun.

AUGUST 4, 2006/8:25 A.M.

CLAY SPANGLER ARRIVES IN CHICAGO AND GOES GULFING IN MEXICO

STAYING UP THAT LATE was a new experience for Chita. She slept several hours past her normal wake-up time the next morning. She might have slept even longer if it wasn't for a phone call from Danny.

"Good morning, Frankie! I've got more good news for you. The circus is coming to town and you've got ringside seats. The Edensgate Circus caravan hit the road early this morning for the Chicagoland Track. It should be there in a few hours."

"Oh, goody. I'll be sure to have my best clown suit starched and pressed."

"Dom and J.D. are in the lead car since they know the way."

"What did Agent McMillan say about the evidence you turned over to him?"

"His reaction was pretty much the same as

yours and mine. He was disappointed, but since he knows beans about corn just like us, he passed it along to someone at the FBI who might be able to make more of its significance."

"What did they find in Fahlgren's workshop?"

"Funny you should ask. You won't believe this, but when the storm hit, it knocked out all the power to the building. Since Fahlgren had been away so long, all of the back-up battery systems were dead. So, at this point they can't figure out how to get past the electronic security systems to get into the building. Fahlgren was a very secretive guy."

"They should figure it out before too long. I mean, the FBI has access to everything, right?"

"Apparently they don't. They flew in a couple of experts yesterday, and they were stumped."

"This may sound too simple, but why not just throw a rock through a window?"

"That is too simple. When the systems failed, all the windows were shuttered with titanium shutters."

"Wow! Fahlgren must have left something pretty important inside that building."

"Our hope is that his paranoia was warranted and we find something good inside."

"Chita says her grandfather still sends him money to continue his work. Could you contact him and ask where Fahlgren is so we can find out what is in the building?"

"If Fahlgren is in the U.S. and receiving payments, he's not paying taxes. The FBI was all over that in a heartbeat. He hasn't paid a dime in taxes since he left the farm. He paid all the taxes he owed to the government during the time he had a work record, so there's nothing the IRS can do to help us. As far as we know, he's not a U.S. citizen, so there's not much we can do."

"What did Chita's grandfather say?"

"He won't return calls."

"What if I could get Chita to call him and ask?"

"I guess it's worth a try. By the way, Clay Spangler landed at O'Hare earlier this morning. But, he got a call from his people in the Gulf about a leaking oil rig, so he hopped a flight to supervise the problem himself."

I shrugged my shoulders. "It must be nice to have a private jet. He's got oil money to burn, and he can go anywhere he wants at the drop of his genuine Texan cowboy hat."

A serious look crossed Danny's face. "Do you think it's safe to take Chita to the track?"

"McMillan seems to think they have this under control. It appears the shooter was the big threat to Chita. You'll have lots of help at the track in Chicago because we have good relations with the police next door in Cicero who owe us some favors."

"What kind of friends?"

"Softball buddies on the Cicero police force. They're the best kind."

"Okay. I'll let Chita know you got her a get-out-of-jail-free card so she can see her horse and dogs. She needs to get back to her regular routine."

Danny hung up the phone, and I stood to go tell Chita. But she must've heard my phone ring because she was standing in our bedroom door-way wondering what the call was about. When I broke the good news to her, she was so happy she started to cry. I told her we'd go to the track around noon so we could meet the caravan and get Dandyosa settled into his stall.

AUGUST 4, 2006/1:45 P.M.
CHITA'S SECURITY BLANKET

IT WAS GREAT TO watch the reunion of Chita with Dandyosa and her dogs, Sheriff and Mary. It was a lovefest with lots of wagging tails and excited prancing and dancing. Chita was back to her old self in an instant. She gave her mother a hug and a kiss and then took charge of her stable hands.

Lola and I thanked Dom and J.D. for rounding up the shooter. They thanked me for getting them a cushy assignment. I introduced them to the crew from the Cicero Police Department, but they knew all the Cicero cops from softball, so we were one big, happy, well-armed, heavy-hitting family if anything happened.

Once things settled down, I got a chance to talk with Marguerite privately. "How was your trip?"

Marguerite shrugged her shoulders and laughed. "No surprises ... which is good for a change."

237

"Do you feel this is under control?"

"Yes, but I want you to continue safeguarding Chita until after the race."

"Agreed." We shook hands on it. "I need to ask you a few questions to make sure I understand what has happened. Why did the shooter go off the deep end?"

"Maybe he was turned away at the gate. We have 325 employees on the farm plus their families. Maybe he failed the security-screening process. These people work hard for me, and Hispanic families are tightly bond. If they pass the screening process, they are admitted. But they must leave the farm at 6:00 P.M. I don't know all of my employees personally, much less their relatives."

I didn't press the matter further. Instead, I let Marguerite do her checks.

Since Chita was comfortable in the condo, Lola and I moved out of that unit to one on the floor below so Marguerite could move into the condo with Chita. Since the building was nearly empty, the bank holding company was easy to work with when we added security people to aid their automated security system. Chita brought Mary to stay in the condo. Mary slept at the foot of Chita's bed, and she bayed like a Baskerville hound whenever anyone opened the door to Chita's room. We also installed a laser-beam security system that detected motion outside Chita's door. Mary, the beagle, detected both sound and smells, so we had that covered too.

Sheriff, the Border collie, was Dandyosa's ever-present companion and friend at the racetrack. Security was tight because it was an international race and an Arab prince would be there to watch his horse race. American celebrities were sure to be at the race too.

Chita watched the Sox night games on TV. At dinner, Lola and I continued to tell stories about great White Sox players. When we told Chita Minnie Minoso played for the White Sox for many years and was the only player ever to play professional baseball in seven different decades, she asked if he was a midget player and drew a lot of walks. We all got a big laugh out of that. We wondered if Chita would introduce her mother to the sport of baseball. She told her mother that Ozzie Guillen ate sunflower seeds just like Dandyosa and herself.

The White Sox jersey became part of Chita's daily wardrobe. Chita's tutor came to Dandyosa's stall every day, and she didn't fall behind in her studies. The regularity of Chita's daily routines were her security blankets. And, watching White Sox play, became an enjoyable part of Chita's routine. She was learning to have fun. As far as I was concerned, we were covered. No one was going to get to Chita on our watch.

HORSING AROUND WITH ROYALTY

THE WEEK PASSED UNEVENTFULLY. Dandyosa was one of the first horses to arrive for the Gold Stakes Race. But, over the next few days, horses began to arrive from around the world. When horses from different countries are together, there are no language barriers like people have. Horses seem to be able to communicate instantly. There were horses from the United Arab Emirates, Argentina, France, Ireland, Great Britain, New Zealand, and Japan—and they all spoke the same language … horse. The owners, trainers, and jockeys needed translators to communicate, but the horses didn't. The horses went about their business and needed no introductions. Maybe there was a positive side to having a limited amount of intelligence and vocal ability. There were no arguments or disputes between the horses. They understood each other and became a harmonious group with a natural pecking order.

The owners acted like peacocks, each preening to appear more important than the other. There were princes, dukes, earls, and a Canadian hockey coach from the state of New York. The owners spent millions on their horses, but in most cases, it wasn't the dollars spent that won races. It was a combination of the owner choosing the right trainer, the right jockey, and the right track; along with the right weather and the track conditions.

The horses' starting positions were the only variable left to chance that the owners couldn't control. But the most important factor would be the mood of each horse when the field came out of the starting gate and vied for positions. Then it was up to the horses.

Each owner was confident his or her horse would win. The owners were very wealthy and only one would go home a winner and tell the story of how he or she knew their horse would win the race. The owners were more interested in bragging rights than winning big purses. Once the race was over, the horses probably didn't care one way or the other. Most of the horses only thought about eating, drinking water, and running.

But Dandyosa was protective of Chita; in his way he loved her and was bonded to her. I thought back to the police horse that convinced me to become a cop. That horse changed my life without ever saying a single word. His nobility did the talking.

The jockeys were also an interesting group. Since this was a stakes race, they were the best of the best and each was a millionaire. They were all incredible athletes that faced great danger each and every time they raced.

Each had broken bones and gone through hours of rehabilitation and sacrifice. They had to consider each and every bite of food and drink they put into their bodies because each ounce they weighed needed to be accounted for. They led a Spartan life and worked for the wealthiest and most socially prominent people in the world. They were small but tough-minded. Some jockeys were hungrier to win than others, and that made a horserace unpredictable.

At the highest levels, jockeys would be crazy to take a bribe over a share of the purse. Ramon Arroyo, like Dandyosa, had something that set him apart and made him special.

I believed Ramon would give Dandyosa a good chance to win. The star jockeys were constantly flown from track to track. Only one local jockey was scheduled to race in the Gold Stakes Race. But when the day of the race came around, other local Chicago jockeys would get to ride against some of the greatest jockeys in the world in the day's undercard races. It was their opportunity to steal the spotlight.

I felt we had enough security at the track and had the home-field advantage. I hoped I was right and that we weren't being lulled into another sneak attack. Miguel Montanayo remained in a cell in Danny's station for safe-keeping.

While I wasn't allowed to meet with Montanayo, Danny gave me regular updates on him. Since being arrested, he was sullen and seldom talked to anyone. He declined representation by an attorney. He seemed resigned to accept his fate for the murders he committed. Since he contemplated committing suicide, he was kept under constant watch. Danny had Spanish-speaking police detectives try to question Montanayo about the murder of undercover agent Johnny Rice and the man with the gold tooth. Montanayo denied having ever met either man. Plus we knew those murders took place at the same time he was at the Tijuana racetrack, so we didn't pursue it further. He was a doomed man, and he chose to accept his fate rather than fight it.

FBI Agent McMillan decided to remain on the Farm of the Future until they gained entrance to Fahlgren's research facility. The FBI was afraid the facility might have some sort of self-protective explosive device inside it, so their work proceeded with great caution. Whatever Fahlgren created must have been very important to command this many security lockouts.

McMillan accepted the document about the hybrid corn, but never told me if it was of any value to him or the case.

I didn't expect him to tell me anything, but I always hoped for the best.

Lola and Chita stuck together while I tried to make myself invisible as I kept watch for trouble.

A LEAK IN THE PIPELINE

CHITA WAS LOOKING FORWARD to seeing her father. He was on a flight that would land at O'Hare early in the morning. As soon as his flight landed, Clay Spangler was alerted that his oil leak in the Gulf was more serious than expected. The oil leak was an ecological disaster for the people who earned their livelihoods fishing in the Gulf. His public relations man made Clay look like a hero instead of an oilman when he filmed Clay running to catch a flight to fix "the mess" himself. His flight was cleared for take-off immediately.

Personally, I thought drilling in the Gulf was a big mistake. When it came to ecology, Clay had a poor record. This was his third leak in three years. Clay tried to spin an ecology message to the public. On the verge of reporting a third straight quarter of record profits to his investors, he wanted to avoid any bad publicity that might hurt Spangler Oil Company's stock price. So,

Clay put on his cowboy hat and promised to fix the leak.

Now that Montanayo was behind bars, his concern for Chita's safety seemed to have vanished. Either that or he trusted Lola and me so completely, he knew we would protect her. I didn't want to believe his interest in making money outweighed his daughter's safety, but he was a difficult man to read. If Chita was my daughter, I would have stayed with her. Even though, she wasn't mine. I liked her and cared about her, and I would have stayed with her until after the race whether we got paid or not. Besides, I always finish any job I start.

Deep down inside, I had an uneasy feeling that there were still a lot of loose ends to be wrapped up. So, Lola and I took Chita to the racetrack each day and remained with her wherever she went for the next couple weeks. Going to the track every day and working behind the scenes was not as exciting as being in the grandstands watching the races. A twelve- to sixteen-hour workday was standard at the track, just like it was at the farm. The work that went on behind the scenes was endless. Thoroughbreds were athletes, and everything they did was monitored. They all needed constant care and attention.

Since the Gold Stakes Race was a big race, reporters and camera crews were already around, doing interviews and creating stories about everything from the horses, the trainers, the jockeys, and the owners; to the cooks that catered the food for the clubhouse. Chita became the center of attention for the media because a thirteen-year-old girl training a million-dollar colt was a great human interest story. She remained humble and answered questions intelligently.

As race day approached, it got increasingly harder to keep Chita out of the public eye. Even though she was thirteen, she was growing into a beautiful woman who photographed well. Dandyosa had a lot of natural personality too. Some animals like cameras and others don't even notice them. When Chita smiled, Dandyosa also turned on the charm. As a result, he commanded a lot of attention. Street vendors outside the track sold Chita t-shirts and Dandyosa t-shirts; both shirts were popular with the crowd. Sales for Clay Spangler t-shirts were slow because they read: "I Fixed the Leak!"

The good news was that Chita wasn't fazed by the attention. She still worked hard every day, got dirty, and sweated. The only change she made to her routine was listening to each day's White Sox game. She became a die-hard Sox fan and wore the jersey Lola bought for her every day. Dandyosa seemed to like listening to the games too. Because Dandyosa was an all-black horse with four white socks, their conversion to becoming White Sox fans was a natural and inevitable thing. Once the South-Siders saw Chita's Guillen 13 jersey, vendors started making Chita 13 jerseys. South-Siders loved her work ethic too. Dandyosa was an underdog with the expert handicappers— but not with Chita.

AUGUST 24, 2006/5:00 A.M.
FOURTEEN CANDLES

THE MORNING OF AUGUST 24th got off to an earlier start than usual. Marguerite came downstairs to wake us up and invite us to Chita's surprise birthday party. It not only would be a surprise for Chita, it was a surprise for us. Marguerite was already dressed to the nines in a summer dress, nylons, high heels, and a full complement of jewelry. Lola and I hurriedly got dressed and went upstairs.

The two police detectives outside the door quietly let us in the condo, where most of the stable hands had already assembled. A big birthday cake with candles was on the table. Marguerite lit the candles and quietly gathered us around the door to Chita's room. As soon as Marguerite opened the door, we all yelled, "Surprise!" In response, her beagle bayed. Then Chita's alarm clock went off, adding to the chaos. But, Sheriff remained calm and wagged his tail in approval. It wasn't how I would want to wake up on my birthday, but Chita woke with a smile. We all sang "Happy Birthday" and then she blew out the candles. We took the cake back into the kitchen so Chita could get dressed in private.

When we were in the kitchen, I asked Marguerite if it was a Brazilian birthday custom to start the day with a birthday cake.

"No," she answered. "But, I like to make each of Chita's birthdays a day filled with surprises, so she will always remember them. That is why I make each one different."

Lola approved. "Wow! That's a great idea! I wish we would have known it was her birthday, we would have gotten her a present."

"That's another surprise. Chita only gets one present for each birthday. It needs to be a special surprise, too, so she will remember it."

Chita came out of her bedroom, followed by Mary and Sheriff, who were as excited about the prospect of getting a piece of birthday cake as I was. Marguerite lit the candles a second time, which was another surprise, and said, "This year you get to make a second wish."

Chita smiled like a second wish was the best present ever, and she blew out the candles again. "Thank you, thank you," she said to everyone.

Marguerite hugged her and said, "Wishes cost nothing, but they are important."

Chita nodded in agreement. "Last year, my

mother covered my birthday cake with black ants. They were plastic, but it was a surprise I'll never forget!"

Everyone laughed and clapped in appreciation of the surprise.

Lola asked, "What did you wish for last year?"

Chita said, "I wished that my mom would never put ants on my cake again."

We all laughed again, and began a day that would be filled with good surprises.

AUGUST 24, 2006/9:14 A.M.
HOW BIG OF A COFFIN
DO YOU NEED FOR A HORSE?

I HAD JUST FINISHED mucking out Dandyosa's stall when I had an unexpected phone call on my cell. The number looked familiar, so I answered it. "Hello?"

"Detective Turk, it's Coroner McGoonin. Do you have a second?"

"Sure. This is a surprise. Are you looking for a hot tip on a trifecta bet for the big race?"

"No, I'm not a betting man. Actually, I'm pretty conservative, for the most part."

"Then to what do I owe the pleasure of your call?"

"Well, things are always slow in the unincorporated area I serve. But, I like to feel like I earn my money, so I've continued putting my Spanish skills to good use by staying in touch with the Mexican authorities in Tijuana. They are a hard-working bunch, and we've developed a good working relationship."

"You're still working on the case of the dead jockey?"

"Like I said, I like to earn my money. I got a call that may shed some light on the things that have happened. The ownership of the horse that was shot may have some bearing on your case."

"How so?"

"Well, there is an organized group of criminals in Mexico that have recently come into power. They are the new *Bourgeoisie*."

"That's French, isn't it?

"Yeah, but this group is the new class of rich in Mexico. I don't know what else to call them."

"A horse by any other color … ?"

"You got it. They are drug thugs. And they have more money than they know what to do with. Since they are the newly rich, they want to appear to be legitimate businessmen; so, in addition to their illegal businesses, they set up legitimate companies to launder some of their money. It is also an effort to try to establish ongoing business relationships with legitimate businessmen and make investments with them."

"So, where is this going, coroner?"

"Did you know Clay Spangler had a mistress in Mexico?"

"No. But my guess is she lives somewhere on the Gulf because he is constantly flying there."

"Good guess, detective. But, she doesn't live there any longer. In fact, the authorities think she's dead. She was mixed up with these drug thugs."

"You are a really good coroner! You know where all the bodies are buried."

"Not this one. She has been missing for several weeks. Her mother notified the authorities."

"Her mother?"

"The mother lived with her daughter. I guess it's better living in a mansion on the Gulf than a hovel in the inner city. It turns out that her daughter owned a part interest in the horse that was shot in Tijuana. When the Tijuana police tried to get in contact with her about the horse, her mother reported that her daughter was missing. She told the police that the last time she saw her daughter, Clay Spangler had taken her out on his yacht for a short cruise, but they never returned."

"Shades of *Gilligan's Island*," I mused.

McGoonin asked the eternal question, "Ginger or Mary Ann? Which would Clay Spangler choose?"

I smiled. "Probably both. He seems to be a greedy guy."

"I agree. Clay Spangler bought the horse for her."

"Tit for tat?"

"I imagine. Does any of this information help you?"

"I'm smiling so much, my cheeks are cramping."

"Drink some Gatorade. You need more salt."

"Thanks for the advice, coroner."

As I hung up the phone, my odds of solving the case suddenly were better than an even money bet.

AUGUST 24, 2006/11:07 A.M.
THERE'S CLAY IN THE GULF

THE NEXT TIME MY phone rang it was a number I didn't recognize. I thought about ignoring it, but the only people who had my number were people who I had given it to, so I answered it. "Frankie Turk."

"Good morning, Turk. This is Clay Spangler."

"Well, this is a surprise. I didn't recognize the number. Where are you?"

"You know how it is with these satellite phones. They give you a new and better model every few weeks. Just when you learn to use one, they give you a more complicated one."

"Where are you, Mr. Spangler?"

"Well, Frankie, I could give you a longitude and latitude, but that's about all. I'm on an oil rig in the Gulf of Mexico. We got a big mess out here. Did you know there are active pirates in the Gulf? They seem to have sabotaged this rig. How'd you like to be head of security for my oil rigs?"

"How's the night life out there?"

"There is no night life. We work around the clock trying to stop the leak. Then, when we fix it, we work around the clock pumping oil."

"Sounds like a great offer, but I don't like working nights and I'm not much of a swimmer. I think I'll stay right where I'm at and keep guarding your daughter."

"She's not answering her cell phone. Is she within your sight?"

"She sure is. She might have forgotten to take her phone with her this morning. It's her birthday, you know."

There was an awkward pause. Then he said, "I know it's her birthday. Could you give her your phone so I can wish her Happy Birthday?"

"Sure." I walked over to Chita and handed her my phone. "It's your dad."

Chita quickly took the phone and had a long conversation with her father. I didn't have a satellite phone with the latest battery that cost over a thousand dollars. I made do with a free phone from my service provider. I hoped the battery didn't die in the middle of their conversation because that would probably anger Clay even more. They talked for over half an hour, which was sort of surprising to me. When Clay was at the farm, he didn't spend much time with Chita. When she finished, she gave me my phone.

"So, what did your dad get you for your birthday?"

Chita beamed. "He named an oil rig after me!"

"He named an oil rig Chita?"

"No. He named it 824 930 1107. And the great part is that's the number of his new satellite phone, too, so I won't forget his phone number!" I was sure I looked confused, so Chita kept talking. "I never remember his phone number, so this is really great. 8/24 is my birthday; 93 is the year of my birth. Zero is the hour I was born (right after midnight) at 11 minutes and 07 seconds after the hour. You'll hear my mom tell the story tonight at dinner, like she does on every one of my birthdays. Dad always says he'll never forget the moment I was born. So, this was a really great gift!"

I smiled and said, "Now you just need to remember to put your phone in your pocket and turn it on."

Lola approached. "What's up, birthday girl?"

"My dad named an oil rig after me."

"That's nice." Lola did not sound impressed.

"I've got to tell Dandyosa! Frankie can tell you all about it."

Chita turned and ran off to tell Dandyosa and her dogs the good news. They would be happy to see her, but they wouldn't have a clue what she was talking about. The animals loved her so much, it didn't matter what she was excited about. They just picked up on her vibe.

Lola looked just as confused as I had moments earlier. "Why would a fourteen-year-old girl be happy about having an oil rig named after her? For her birthday present?"

"It's named 824 930 1107—the same number as her father's new cell phone."

"What is so great about that?"

"It will be easier for her to remember."

Lola asked, "Why would that number be easier for her to remember?"

"It is the date of her birth 8/24/93 and the time of her birth midnight (zero hour/11 minutes and 7 seconds after the hour). Chita said Marguerite will tell the story of Chita's birth tonight at dinner."

"Darn it! Now you wrecked our dinner surprise story."

I looked at Lola and smiled.

"Why are you smiling at me, Frankie?"

"I just remembered something. What was the number of the post office box we got our assignment from?"

"I don't know."

"824. Chita's birthday. Surprised?"

"Yes. That number is special to Clay. Do you think Clay gave us this assignment instead of Marguerite?"

That was something I hadn't considered before. "Wow! I guess I always assumed it was Marguerite, but as far as the case goes, it does make more sense that Clay would be the one to hire us. He's the one who wheels and deals all over the world and attracts attention by stirring the pot. He'd be the one who might be worried someone might want to kidnap his daughter. He's got leg men putting out fires for him around the world. Maybe one of Clay's leg men in Chicago hired the man with the gold tooth to put our letter in the post office box and take us out to Stickney to find the dead jockey."

Lola nodded her head in agreement and smiled. "That makes sense. I went into that post office a thousand times and I never would have guessed Johnny Rice was really an undercover cop. He looked pretty pathetic. Probably Gold Tooth needed Johnny's wheelchair and couldn't bribe him, so maybe he hit Johnny on the head a little too hard. After all, Johnny was on his last legs—or leg."

"I could buy that, Lola. Then Gold Tooth dumped Johnny's body in a dumpster figuring nobody would miss another homeless bum. When the police found the body and realized a cop got bumped off, word got out on the street. Then, whoever hired Gold Tooth had to bump him off to eliminate the possibility of him telling the police who had hired him. As we know, Gold Tooth was a talkative guy. He would have sung like a canary if the cops found him alive. That's why rich guys have leg men. If something goes wrong, the rich guy is removed from direct contact with the leg man. His actions are a communication breakdown or a misunderstanding instead of a crime."

"That's definitely true. When we first got hired, we were hired to be bodyguards. That was our only job. It was going to be easy money. We were going to take turns painting each other's toenails."

"That was never going to happen. But, continue your train of thought."

"But, lots of unexpected things started to happen—and, looking back on it, all the pieces fell together too easily. We were asked to keep Chita safe and keep an eye out for kidnappers. Maybe the dead bodies were just distractions to throw us off the trail. We've been looking for kidnappers that don't exist." Lola shrugged her shoulders. "Let's keep our game faces on, like we don't know anything, and see what develops. I don't think there's any threat to Chita."

"Do you think Dom, J.D., and you can keep Chita safe from harm while I go see Danny?" I asked.

"Since there is nobody to protect her from, I think we'll do a great job. But, don't worry, we won't let our guard down."

AUGUST 24, 2006/12:00 P.M.
HOLY HOT DOGS, BATMAN!

I ARRIVED AT DANNY'S door just in time for lunch. "It's your turn to buy lunch, Danny."

"But, you have an expense account."

"Hopefully not for much longer. I think we're about to wrap this one up. The suspects are dropping like flies. What do you have a taste for?"

"How about hot dogs and fries?"

Danny and I got into his Crown Vic, activated the flashing lights and siren, and drove to Christ's Dog House on Halsted in record time. It is a walk-up place with no indoor access. They hand the food to you through a screened window that opens. The screen is supposed to keep the flies out, but they get in anyway because the dogs and fries are that good. The customers don't mind the flies because flies don't eat much and steamed dogs and fries boiled in oil are pretty germ-free. It is a favorite hangout of high school kids with acne and tattoos who wear wool ski caps in both summer and winter—as a fashion statement and a territorial warning. The chefs at Christ's put enough salt on the fries to raise your blood pressure to unsafe levels, and the fries drip with oil, which makes them go down easy. A Chicago dog is pure beef with mustard (no ketchup), relish, raw onions, a kosher pickle wedge, two hot peppers, and celery salt. The bun is brown on the outside, white on the inside, and soft. They sell Coke, Hires Root Beer, and Green River (lime soda that has been made in Chicago in limited quantities for over 100 years). If you ask, they'll even make you a Green River float that is guaranteed to float your boat.

Danny ate and talked at the same time, which was awful to look at, but I was used to it. "So, you look happy, Frankie. You got something for me?"

"You bet. I got you a big stack of napkins in case you drip oil on your tie."

"Funny! When I bring my mother to Christ's, she does the same thing." He took a napkin from me and wiped the oil off his fingers. "Continue."

I related everything Lola and I discussed. It all made sense to Danny too. McGoonin's investigation supported what we discovered. And, since Clay Spangler was miles away from these happenings in every instance, there was no chance he could be linked to anything—which was the way these things were generally done. There were lots of leg men who weren't very smart and thought murder for hire was an easy way to make a fast buck. Gold Tooth didn't have any money on him when they found him in the flophouse; so whoever "gaveth" also "tooketh away." We didn't know who killed the jockey, but since he was a nobody, nobody was going to go looking for his murderer. But, as luck would have it, Lola found the cell phone and McGoonin had a lot of time on his hands. Danny said Pedro tried to get the shooter to confess, but the shooter told him he was afraid for his family in Mexico. So that was a dead end too.

After we ate every bite of our dogs and fries, we cooled off by washing them down with Green River floats. Then, I told Danny about our "number" discovery.

"So, you think Clay is a numerologist?"

"Indubitably. He has billions of dollars; I bet he recalls how he earned each one. Has the FBI figured out how to get into Fahlgren's lab yet?"

"No. Would you like to pass this number along to McMillan? I promised him I'd share information when and if I got it."

"Well, at the risk of feeling stupid if I'm wrong, I don't know what I can lose by giving it to him."

"You have looked stupid before and survived," said Danny. "But, I bet the odds are you'll likely come up a winner if you pass the number along. Just don't bet it on the lottery."

"True. Let's call him."

Danny called McMillan, who answered on the first ring.

"McMillan."

"This is Danny, Agent McMillan. I'm having lunch with Frankie Turk. He thinks he might have discovered a solution to your dilemma."

"How so?"

"He's a private detective, but he's willing to share. Would you like to speak with him?"

McMillan listened to everything I said, but he never said a word. I sensed that he wrote the number down. When I finished talking, he asked to speak with Danny again. I don't know what he said, but it must have been short and sweet because Danny smiled and hung up.

As I hit the bottom of the Green River float, I got air instead of liquid. "What did McMillan say?"

He said, "'Son of a bitch! How did you come up with that number?'"

CHITA AND MARGUERITE EACH TAKE THE CAKE, AGAIN

MARGUERITE PAID THE CATERING service at the track to stay late and throw a surprise birthday party for Chita. Everyone from the stable was invited. Since Lola and I were Chita's bodyguards, we told Chita we were taking a shortcut to her mother's car so we could get home for her party. We went through the back door of the track kitchen, and when we opened the door to a banquet room, Chita got another unexpected birthday surprise when everyone shouted, "Surprise!" It caught her off guard, but when she saw all of the people she was really happy that they wanted to celebrate her birthday with her. There was a Mariachi band that provided happy music and the spread of food included Chita's favorite healthy foods. Even though it was her birthday, she didn't change her healthy eating habits. However, she did allow herself to have a second piece of birthday cake.

No one was allowed to bring Chita a gift except her mother. Instead people made donations to the Chicago Anti-Cruelty Society, which made Chita very happy. When the time came for Chita to open her gift, everyone wondered what the daughter of a billionaire would receive. In keeping with the rest of the day, the present was a really big surprise. Chita opened a white box with a black ribbon around it. Inside was an Ozzie Guillen White Sox jersey with the number 14 on it. Chita looked confused and said, "Ozzie's number is 13."

"And you were thirteen up until today," said her mother. "But I checked, and Ozzie Guillen is forty-one years old, and now you are fourteen, which is forty-one in reverse, so now you have a special Ozzie jersey that no one else has. Surprise!"

Everyone laughed, applauded, and sang "Happy Birthday" to Chita. Soon after, they shook Chita's hand and went home. While Marguerite was in the kitchen paying the caterers, Chita asked us why her mother thought the number on the jersey referred to her age. Lola gave Chita some good advice: "I don't know why she thought that, but I think you should wear it anyway, because it was a surprise. If people ask why you have an Ozzie Guillen jersey with 14 on it, tell them you didn't want anyone to mistake you for Ozzie."

Chita thought she'd get a lot of laughs with that answer, so she decided to wear it instead of the 13 jersey, because it was a thoughtful gift that she'd never forget.

It's funny, but no matter how hard I tried, I couldn't remember what I had received for my fourteenth birthday. Maybe Marguerite's unorthodox child-rearing techniques had some merit. The passing of a birthday is only one day, but it is a significant day that completes another year of a person's life. What would Chita's fourteenth year be like?

AUGUST 25, 2006/10:50 A.M.
A LONG AWAITED LEAK

MIDWAY AIRPORT IS LESS than five miles from the Chicagoland Track. Agent McMillan sent an FBI agent to pick me up at the racetrack and drive me to Midway where a private airplane was waiting for me. I asked lots of questions on the ride to the airport, but I got no answers. I boarded the plane, and it took off immediately. There was no flight attendant to teach me how to fasten my seatbelt, instruct me in the location of the emergency exits, or offer me a beverage and peanuts. It took a little over an hour for us to land at The Farm of the Future.

McMillan greeted me as I got off the airplane. "How was your flight?"

"How come there were no miniature liquor bottles?" I asked.

"I wanted you sober. Let's take a ride to Fahlgren's lab."

McMillan drove. There was not substantive

talk on the way. When we reached the lab, there were armed guards everywhere.

"We've tried every way we can think of to get past this security system," Said McMillan.

"Did you try saying please?"

"Not funny. We have decided to give your code a try. We wanted you to be here when we tried it."

"In case it blows up?"

"Exactly. I'm going to use you as a shield."

A serious-looking man in a military bomb suit waddled up to me and introduced himself. "My name is Morton Duncan. I am an explosives specialist. How did you come by this password?"

"First, let me say that I'm not sure it *is* a password—but it *is* a number that has special meaning to Clay Spangler, who owns this property. It is his satellite phone number and it is the date and time of his daughter's birth—her birthday was yesterday. As a birthday present, he named an oil rig in the Gulf of Mexico and this number is the exact time of her birth."

"Anything else?"

"When I began working as a bodyguard for the family, my down payment was put in a post office box that started with the three numbers of his daughter's birthday. Mr. Spangler is a busy man. To simplify his life, I think he uses this number almost like a universal pass key."

Morton Duncan did not react to a word I

said. He handed me a piece of paper, which he held with very thick gloves. "Is this the correct sequence of the numbers?"

I examined it and said, "Yes. But, I'm not sure if it is continuous or if there are spaces."

"Fair enough. If this sequence was created by Clay Spangler, why do you assume it will open Fahlgren's lab?"

"Good question. Spangler hated Fahlgren and closed down his facility. I think Spangler might have taken great pleasure in changing the password so Fahlgren could never enter his own lab again."

"Makes sense to me. Here goes nothing." Morton motioned for all of us to take cover, so we moved away. He gingerly used the eraser end of a pencil to punch the code into the number pad. He had radio contact with McMillan, and he said the numbers aloud as he punched in the code. We all held our breath as he paused before punching in the last digit. As he did, he said, "Open Sesame Street!" Either Morton had a great sense of humor, or he had never read *Tales of the Arabian Nights*.

A loud click startled everyone, and then the titanium shutters rolled up and the door to the lab clicked open. A stench wafted out of the building. Four years is a long time for a building to be closed. It was like the building belched the smell of rotting garbage. The ever-conservative Agent Thomas McMillan immediately called for gas masks. We all put one on and entered the building. A technical team quickly figured out how to restore the power, and the lights soon flickered on. We could begin our search of the building.

McMillan had a floorplan, so he and I went straight to Fahlgren's office. The stench increased as we got closer to Fahlgren's office. When McMillan opened the door, we immediately determined that the stench was coming from a gooey substance that had been contained in a large glass beaker which had shattered. Over time, whatever the beaker contained had slowly melted and now oozed over the sides of Fahlgren's desk and onto the carpet.

FBI technicians booted-up the computer, and they all came to life, exchanging information and updating themselves. I'm not a computer expert, but these computers looked like relics from another time and place. One of the technicians was concerned that they might fail to restart, but when they did, he seemed pleased. He gingerly worked his way around Fahlgren's desk to the keyboard and did a quick perusal of Fahlgren's files.

McMillan patted me on the back and gave me a thumb's up. He motioned for me to follow him out of the office. He escorted me downstairs and back outside. We took off our gas masks, and he said, "Thanks. I'll have someone fly you back to Midway."

"Now?"

"Yes, right now. Your work is done here."

"Can't I stay and see what you find?"

"No."

"But, you'll tell me later?"

"No."

"So, I'll have to read about it in the newspapers?"

"No."

"Why?"

"The FBI needs to know more than the public. It keeps us a step ahead."

An FBI agent who was much bigger than me opened a door to a car and motioned for me to climb in. Five minutes later, I was on my way back to Midway Airport. Once again, there were no refreshments onboard. But, I did avail myself of the facilities, and I urinated on the toilet seat just to show the FBI who was the boss.

FAST TIMES AND HIGH STAKES

THE DAYS THAT FOLLOWED my quick trip to the farm were festive ones. It was a special week of racing at Chicagoland Track, with the world's best horses and riders getting ready for the Gold Stakes Race. Dandyosa was not considered to be a serious contender for the Gold Stakes Race, but Chita became a media favorite because a teenage girl training a racehorse is the stuff Disney movies are made of.

Chita was a natural on camera and her genuine naiveté was charming. She was asked to do lots of television interviews. The hardworking, blue-collar daughter of two billionaires was a refreshing story for the media. Everywhere Chita went, she wore her #14 Ozzie Guillen White Sox jersey and gushed about the Sox. Since the Sox were always underdogs, and Chita was always in the company of her dogs, the Sox attendance increased as the team entered the dog days of summer, which hopefully would boost the team's morale for the stretch run.

At the Chicagoland Track, Chita and Dandyosa were the sentimental fan favorites. Since the race was only a few days off, there was a feeling of excitement in the air because the dark horse, Dandyosa, would be tested for the first time. It is rare that newspapers devote a lot of space to horse racing, but the human-interest angle of Chita and Dandyosa was a powerful story. While the fans loved the concept of a teenager training a racehorse, they did not put their money where their hearts were, and Dandyosa seemed destined to go off at 15-1 odds.

Clay Spangler still had not arrived in Chicago, but the press eagerly awaited his arrival. In anticipation and celebration of the last big weekend of the summer, all of the gasoline companies raised gas prices to take advantage of the increased travel needs of consumers. Since Clay Spangler was going to be in Chicago for the race, he was going to be the public's whipping horse for the oil industry. His publicity department tried to keep the leaking oil well in the Gulf out of the news, but it became front page news, and Spangler was attacked by the press as an enemy of the world's ecosystem and a shameless profiteer.

Unbeknownst to Marguerite, a reporter tried to gain access to The Farm of the Future, but the reporter was quickly shooed away by the FBI. Since she couldn't write a story about the environmentally friendly farm, she wrote a cover story about the FBI's investigation of Spangler Oil, which meant more negative publicity for the Spangler family. This greatly angered Marguerite, and it was sure to cause greater tension between her and Clay when he returned. But nothing seemed to bother Chita. She was determined not to deviate from her daily tasks and her goal of winning the Gold Stakes Race.

America's economy bottomed out during the summer of 2006. A lavish festival of racing some of the greatest horses in the world seemed out of place. In Chicago, many families lost their homes. Some people would gamble money they couldn't afford to lose. The wealthiest people and the poorest people were worlds apart that year. During the Great Depression there was a horse called SeaBiscuit. He gave the nation hope. Maybe Dandyosa and Chita would lift the nation's spirits too.

The leg men we met on this case were desperate men. They killed without remorse. Clay was the worst of them because he killed the Gulf and maritime jobs of many people, and may have caused irreparable damage to the ecosystem.

Lola and I were never big gamblers. Some cops frequently gamble, but most of them lose. Lola and I never liked to take chances. When Lola fought off the attack on the farm, she played it safe and won. But, we made an exception when we both placed our bets on Dandyosa. When the reporters asked Chita how much money she had put on Dandyosa, she told the reporters that she just turned fourteen and couldn't bet legally. For Chita, the most important thing about the race was Dandyosa winning.

Betting is a slippery slope. Betting taints sports. In all Major League Baseball locker rooms, a sign hangs above the doors that lead to the field. It reads: "No Betting Allowed." Pete Rose ignored the sign, and he developed a gambling sickness that resulted in him being banned from baseball forever—even though he was one of the greatest players ever.

Betting frequently turns into an addiction. When I was seven years old, I watched a leg man take the keys of our next-door neighbor's wife's new 1957 pink-and-black Chevrolet convertible and drive it away because he couldn't cover his bet. He learned the hard way. So, I didn't tell Lola what I bet, and she didn't tell me what she bet.

Lola and I bet on Dandyosa because we didn't want to create bad karma. And that is why we laid down our bets three days before the race. We had no control over the outcome of the race. Win or lose, we would be unemployed in three days. We kept our eyes and ears open, and watched Chita and Dandyosa like hawks. All of our security measures would remain in place.

RACE DAY

RACE DAY BEGAN WITH the arrival of protesters who planned to march in front of the racetrack to complain about Clay Spangler's "Leak in the Gulf!" Agent McMillan refused to release any information about the investigation of The Farm of The Future, but dark clouds seemed destined to gather around the Spanglers on race day. Even the morning weather forecast was cloudy and overcast. While the track would be fast for the first race, everyone wondered if the weather would hold until the Gold Stakes Race, which was scheduled for a 4:00 P.M. post time.

We got word that Clay Spangler's flight landed at O'Hare at 10:00 A.M. But, since he was flying in from Mexico, he landed and deplaned at the International Terminal of O'Hare Field, which was not as convenient to the racetrack as Midway. His limo ride was uneventful, and he arrived at the track just as the gates opened; so the protestors made a big show of his arrival. He was dressed in a blue blazer, khaki-colored pants, a white shirt, and a red-and-blue tie. He smiled for the cameras and the protestors as he walked past; he wanted to make friends not enemies. He assured the television reporters that the leak had been contained and minimal damage had been done to the environment. He promised to voluntarily pay for the cleanup, and apologized for his crew's accident. He noted that Spangler Oil kept America strong by making sure America's demands for oil were met. He kept walking the whole time he was being interviewed, and he quickly ended the interview by saying, "I've said all I'm going to say about oil today. This is my daughter, Chita's, day, not mine." The increased track security made sure no one followed him into the stable area.

When Spangler saw me sitting on a chair in front of Dandyosa's stable, he asked, "Did I hire you to guard my daughter or a horse?"

I got off the chair and greeted him. "Lola is with Chita. She's doing another television interview. She's turning into a media star."

Clay had on his game face, so he smiled and shook my hand. I noted that he had a custom-made White Sox 14 tie tack holding his red-and-blue tie in place. Chita must have told him about her favorite birthday present. He seemed determined not to let anyone ruffle his feathers or spoil his day. He was in command of the situation, and he was amiable and warm. "Good to see you, Turk. For awhile, I thought I was going to miss the race because of that damn leaking oil well. But, I pushed my crews mercilessly and kept them working night and day until we finally got it capped."

"Is that the well you named after your daughter?"

"It is. And it's going to be a big producer."

"Good old 8249301107."

"So, Chita told you the story!"

"Yes. And Chita warned us Marguerite would give us a play-by-play description of her birth—and she did, right down to the second, like the number of the well. Personally, I thought it was touching, but Chita did a fair amount of blushing."

"Which is only natural."

"Not to change the subject, but I hear the Gulf of Mexico is a really rough place to do business these days."

"There's nothing easy about the oil business these days. It used to be you could drill a hole in your backyard in Texas and find oil. Not anymore. It's a constant fight to keep what's yours. You can't take anything for granted. If you turn your back for a second, somebody will try to steal what's yours. Mexico is a very tough place to do business today. Drug lords rule the courts and terrorize the poor people. And, these drug lords have money to burn. So, now they want to get involved in the oil business."

"It's always a case of supply and demand. That is what happened during Prohibition. Everybody wanted booze, but they couldn't have it, so some people bent the rules, gained control of the limited supply, and distributed it in unorthodox ways."

"You're a student of history, Frankie," said Clay. "Good for you! But today's drug dealers are more like terrorists. They make Prohibition seem like the good old days. The Mexican government tries to soft-peddle it, but the Gulf of Mexico is controlled by Mexican pirates who work with the drug lords. Can you believe there are still pirates sailing the seas? And, there is very little that can be done to them since no one has jurisdiction over them. International courts can't intervene. So, these people can do whatever they want and get away with it. Their favorite targets are private yachts. Earlier this summer, pirates boarded my yacht."

"I didn't know that."

"My people managed to keep it out of the papers, but pirates boarded my yacht. I personally know the President of The United States, and even he couldn't help me."

"Were you looking for oil?"

"No. I was having some 'me time' with my mistress. I'm guessing you noted Marguerite's coldness towards me. It's been that way for over five years. What's a man to do?"

"I don't give that kind of advice. But, go on."

"Make no mistake, these people knew who I was, and they knew what they wanted. The oil business is very competitive. I had dinner with an Arab sheik the week before and mentioned my intended tryst. It was stupid of me, and I never should have mentioned it. They frown on that kind of thing. I was pandering to my own ego in the middle of a business deal. I don't know what I was thinking. My guess is the sheik told someone in the oil business in Mexico about it because pirates boarded my yacht as soon as we reached international waters. Have you ever done business with someone from the Middle East? Or China?"

"I've discovered the Chinese are nice to do business with," I said. "They give you fortune cookies with carry-out orders."

"I'm glad you have a sense of humor about this, but when I tell you what these bastards did, I don't think you'll find it so funny. I am not used to being bested. What I am trying to tell you is that I was the victim. They did their homework because they knew everything about me. They planned on blackmailing me. The first thing they told me was they intended to tell Marguerite about my mistress. When I told them Marguerite already knew about my mistress, they threw her overboard to attract sharks. Do you have any idea how awful that was to see?"

"Yes, I do. I'm a cop. I see all sorts of awful things. Look, let's get down to brass tacks. What did they want?"

He hesitated before answering. "They thought I was in possession of a formula Dr. Fahlgren developed in his lab at the farm. I had no idea what they were talking about. I hadn't seen that man in years. My wife idolized him in her college days, and she paid him millions upon millions to build The Farm of the Future and to create natural and biofuel alternatives for the future.

"Personally, I don't care about the future. I live in the here and now. I am in the oil business— not agriculture. So, I called Marguerite and asked her if Fahlgren had developed a formula."

"What did she say?"

"She said he did, but it had nothing to do with energy. I asked her if she would give it to me, and she agreed. But she also said it would be worthless to them."

"Not entirely. It increased the yield of corn by 1.5 percent."

Clay Spangler looked dumbfounded. "Marguerite told you about it—but she didn't tell me?"

"No, she didn't tell me about it. We found the formula on a microchip in a button bag that was sewn on the silks of the dead jockey."

Clay looked stunned. It seemed like he didn't know what to say. He mumbled, "Dead jockey ..."

"Look, you hired us to protect your daughter. When we went to pick up our assignment, a man, who we assume you sent, was waiting outside the post office for us. He took us to see a dead jockey that was dumped in the lake at the bottom of a gravel pit. And, guess what? We eventually linked that jockey to you. So, don't play dumb. It was the jockey who rode the two longshots in Tijuana, back in July. We found the microchip with the formula sewn into his silks. Was that just a coincidence?"

"You've been investigating me?"

"No, not really. While we were protecting your daughter, our investigation uncovered information that led to you. Do you want to know what we discovered while you were globetrotting, cutting deals, and plugging leaks?"

"No. This conversation is over."

"I don't think so. Marguerite sewed the microchip into the silks. The jockey was abducted and driven to the Stickney Quarry. Somebody had to get that microchip into the right hands. But he died before he could deliver it to Dr. Fahlgren. It was a longshot that the coroner found the microchip during his examination of the jockey's silks. I had the microchip translated."

Spangler took a deep breath. "It was very complicated. The Mexican lawyer in Pilsen bought a great horse for the trainer and asked the trainer to remain in Mexico with his nephew. But they were greedy and stupid. They called attention to themselves by winning too many races at long odds. I lost my temper and ordered the shooting of the lawyer's race horse. So they needed to get out of Tijuana in a hurry.

"Marguerite sent them directions to the farm from O'Hare. When they arrived, a limo driver held up a sign that said: "Edensgate Farm." Another man flashed his badge and identified himself as a Chicago undercover police detective. The car he drove was a metallic-blue Barracuda. He boasted he knew a shortcut to the farm and invited the jockey to ride with him. But as soon as the jockey got into the Barracuda he disappeared from sight. The limo driver drove straight to Edensgate, but it was the middle of the night when they arrived, and they were turned away at the gate because they didn't have security clearance. The limo driver dropped the trainer and his bags at a small motel and returned to O'Hare. Unfortunately, the trainer brought his .357 Magnum and plenty of ammunition. He was insulted when he was turned away at the gate, and he devised a plan to attack the farm. The storm made the attack easier. He attacked the guard shack at the height of the storm.

"How in the hell did this get so out of control? My plan was simple and legal. Once we were back in Chicago, I canceled their return tickets with the airline. I also made it difficult for them to clear Customs. The Pilsen lawyer was connected to the Mexican drug dealers. I hate to tell you, but it cost me a fortune to keep this quiet. These people are a major source of drugs for the United States. They have people in every big city. Is it any surprise that they had people in Chicago? Cicero has always been a place for immigrants to settle, and some of them get involved in illegal activities as a fast lane to attain the American dream. My guess is the drug dealers had a welcoming committee greet the jockey at O'Hare. The people they sent probably weren't the smartest; they were the most brutal. Needless to say, they were more intent on giving the kid a beating than finding the microchip. I doubt these guys would have known a microchip from a corn chip. They failed to recover the chip and that is how the jockey ended up dead in the quarry in Stickney. And that's when I hired you to protect my daughter."

"And you hired somebody to take Lola and me out to Stickney?"

"No. Some people who owed me a favor arranged that for me. I trusted the man who they hired treated you well. Were there any problems?"

"Sort of. He was a nice guy with a gift of gab, but it turns out he killed an undercover cop just before he picked us up."

Clay looked genuinely shocked. "What?"

"The guy they hired was a player. Not bright. Your people should have asked for references first. And that's just for starters. Somebody killed him to shut him up."

Clay sounded outraged. "This is a nightmare! Who killed him?"

"We don't know yet. The police are still working on it. And, you already know what the trainer did in Pleasant Ridge and Edensgate."

"Don't try pinning that on me. I had nothing to do with that."

"Well, in a manner of speaking. But, I think you lit his fuse. Why didn't you just fire him?"

"I needed him to ride those races in Mexico and deliver the formula. That was the deal we made."

"Why didn't the gangsters come after you instead?"

"Do you know how many people stand between me and the public? It's easier to kill the president than me. Going off on my yacht with my mistress was a stupid mistake I'll never make again. After the trainer attacked the farm, I sent them the formula. That put an end to the matter."

"So, you don't think you did anything wrong?"

Clay Spangler laughed. "How dumb do you think I am? Do you think I would ever hire someone to commit murder? If anyone ever tried to investigate this matter, there would never be any evidence to link me to any crime. You and

I are very much alike, Mr. Turk. I keep my personal business inside my head where no one can see it. When it comes to personal matters, I am as invisible as you are." He reached into his pocket and pulled out an envelope filled with cash and handed it to me. "Here is your cash payment for services rendered. As soon as the race is over, your work is done, and I will expect both of you to disappear."

"But who will be your daughter's bodyguard?"

"No one. It was just a precaution. No one ever intended to kidnap her."

Behind Spangler, I saw Pedro walking towards us. When Clay sensed Pedro was nearby, he dropped his voice and whispered, "Except, technically you and Lola kidnapped Chita, but I'm certainly not going to press charges against you unless you force me. All these things I just told you are between you and me. You never had any intention of hurting her, did you?"

"You certainly have that right. She is an amazing girl. But, it wasn't our idea to kidnap her. We were asked to do it."

Spangler looked shocked. "By who?"

"Well, I'm not allowed to say because I was sworn to secrecy. But I have a feeling you may meet him in the near future."

Pedro walked up to Clay Spangler and offered his hand. "Hello, Mr. Spangler. Good to see you. This is a big day."

Spangler looked irritated and tried to shoo Pedro away. "Not now. I'm very busy." Another man walked into the stable which irritated Spangler even more. "No visitors. Pedro, get rid of this man."

"I'm sorry, Mr. Spangler. I can't. I work for him."

Thomas McMillan flashed his FBI badge and introduced himself. "Mr. Spangler, I'm Federal Agent Thomas McMillan. We've never met, but I've had you under investigation for the past three years."

"For what?"

"You applied for a bio-energy formula patent that we have proof was stolen from Dr. Peter Fahlgren."

"That's absurd. That formula was created by my staff in a private, secure facility."

Pedro started to talk, "Mr. Spangler ... "

Spangler shot back, "Not now, Pedro. Go away."

Pedro held up his FBI badge and said, "Sorry, sir, but I can't go away. I am a Federal agent, too. Please, come with us. We have some questions we'd like to ask you."

Dandyosa snorted as they escorted Clay Spangler away.

Clay Spangler didn't go to jail. He hired a battalion of lawyers who created endless paperwork.

Since Clay Spangler had more money than the U.S. Treasury, the case was eventually dropped. Thanks to his legions of leg men, there were no direct ties to Clay and any of the murders or the stolen patent. The patent for the biofuel of the future was tied up in court battles that would rage on for years.

But, Clay Spangler didn't have the pleasure of seeing the Gold Stakes Race that afternoon. As soon as he was escorted from the Chicagoland Track by the FBI, the weather took a turn for the better. By race time, there wasn't a cloud in the sky and the temperature was a pleasant seventy-five degrees. The track was fast, and Dandyosa wasn't nervous. Ramon Arroyo was confident.

Lola and I decided to try to beat the odds that favored the track. The maiden stallion, Dandyosa, went off as a 25-1 shot. Since Taylor Street only accepts cash, we bet cash at the track and several other private institutions. Why? Lola felt guilty about sleeping in the bed of the family who lost their home in Bridgeport. We decided to try to win enough money to buy the house back from Taylor Street and give it to the family. But that involved beating the odds. It is always hard to beat the odds.

We didn't bet a lot of money at the track because that would have changed the track odds. But the private institutions offer track odds, too, so we bet Clay's cash on Clay's daughter's horse. Dandyosa drew a nice post position, but he stumbled coming out of the gate. To our disappointment, Dandyosa definitely didn't run his best race. But, on this day, September 1, 2006, at 4:15 P.M., Dandyosa brought the crowd to its feet as he won by a nose, making Chita Spangler the youngest trainer ever to win a stakes race and nearly breaking the track record his first time out.

It's always hard to beat the odds, but Dandyosa managed to do it, as Lola and I watched in wonder.

DENOUEMENT

AT LAST, OUR WORK was done. There was no longer a threat to Chita or Dandyosa. Lola and I collected our winnings in cash as we were wont to do (cash is king), and then walked hand-in-hand towards the front gate of the track.

Danny had sent Mike Phillips to pick us up in my Oldsmobile. It was easy to spot. When we were within earshot of Mike, he smiled and said, "Never accept rides from strangers."

"We're no stranger than you. I prefer to be anonymous. It's safer."

Mike reached into his suit pocket, pulled out an envelope, and handed it to me.

"What's this?" I asked.

"Your new assignment."

"I guess there is no rest for the wicked."

At that moment, an Irish Chicago cop on horseback, sauntered by. "Ain't it the truth?" he said. "You two keep moving."

I swear the horse winked at me.

An excerpt from JoBe Cerny's next book …

THE GREAT DEPRESSIONS OF TUG COLLIER

It was nearly midnight on Friday, March 29, 1931, when I entered a dead-end alley, chasing a man I wanted to kill. I had drawn my .45 and nearly had him cornered when a shot rang out from behind me. The roar of the weapon echoed in the brick canyon that formed the dead-end alley, and I felt a pinch in the center of my spine. I lost all feeling in my arms and legs as the blast knocked me forward. Then I saw my heart explode out of my chest in a red blur as I fell forward and waited to hit the pavement face first—but the impact never came. Instead, I fell into an inky blackness.

Earlier that night, I visited a client on South Indiana Avenue in Chicago, and he paid me in cash. He was an odd bird who kept his stash of cash in an old shoe box under his bed. Like many people during The Great Depression, he didn't believe in savings and loans. I solved a problem for him so he counted out seventy-five C-notes to express his gratitude. Then he fished in his garbage can for a used envelope. Since times were tough, he must have decided to save money by cutting back on paper. Maybe that's how he accumulated so much money. I tucked the pile of smiling Bens face first into the front pocket of my overcoat kissing my .45. It gave me a warm feeling as I headed out into the night of a late winter flurry.

My name is Tug Collier, and I grew up on the west side of Chicago. That's where the mob was and that's where my kind of work was. But, South Indiana Avenue is on the east side of Chicago (go figure). The interesting thing about the east side of Chicago is that it is only a few blocks wide and it only exists on the south side of Chicago. The reason is Lake Michigan is east of the center of Chicago, and the lake is at an angle to the street grid. So there is only a narrow strip of land east of the center of Chicago on the South Side. But on the North Side of Chicago, as you drive north along the lake shore, the land of the east side gradually disappears into the waves of Lake Michigan and is submerged under the water and only the western streets survive. So, the West Side of Chicago is the biggest part of the city. But, if someone was looking for trouble in my day, South Indiana Avenue was the best place to find it. Walking the streets with $7,500.00 cash in my pocket wasn't smart, but I figured my jalopy was parked just outside my client's door. Greta, my girlfriend, a big-boned Swedish natural blonde (both top and bottom she was proud to say) was sitting in the front seat with the motor running (my jalopy's not hers). I figured, "How much trouble can I get into walking down a flight of stairs and getting into my car?"

Walking down the stairs was easy. Greta smiled at me as she saw me walk out my client's door. I smiled back and patted my pocket. She giggled, clapped like a trained seal, and rolled down the car window to greet me with a kiss. I handed her the cash, and she tucked the Bens between her ample bosoms because she was very maternal by nature. As I walked around to the other side of the car, I saw a guy I'd been looking for come out of a speakeasy, and the chase was on. Too bad I went down that alley trying to chase him down.

Anyway, after I was shot, I don't know how long I fell without hitting anything solid. It seemed like I fell forever. I guess I blacked out or fell asleep because I lost track of time. At some point I opened my eyes, but I didn't see anything because there was only darkness. So I closed my eyes and just kept falling. I began to think there would never be an end to my fall. But then, after a very long time, I opened my eyes and saw a small dot of light a long ways off. It wasn't much, but it was better than complete darkness so I focused on it. After all, it was something, and for a long time, I had nothing. The dot of light was as constant as the North Star, so I trusted each time I opened my eyes that it would always be there for me so I could get my bearings. To pass the time, I would close my eyes and dream. I spent a lot of time thinking about what I was—a second rate police detective who lived on the east side of the law in Chicago to supplement my income. I spent a lot of my time working in "No Man's Land" where I was always willing to do anything for anyone who had a buck. I was a man on a mission, and my primary mission was to make money. Because it was the Great Depression, nice people didn't have the bucks, the bad guys did. And since I wasn't particular about who I did business with, it led to my long term predicament.

Then one day, or month, or year, I opened my eyes. The darkness was gone, and I was no longer falling. Instead, I found myself in a room without doors. No lamps were visible in the room, but it had a soft golden white glow. I sat on a chair in front of a table. It reminded me of a nice police station interrogation room. (If there is such a thing.) There was dead silence, and no sign of life. The first thing I did was look down at my chest. I had on a fresh white shirt and a flashy tie. There was no hole in my chest. Somehow, I miraculously still seemed to be in one piece. My .45 was still in my overcoat pocket. My black fedora was still on my head. I remembered I gave my babe the Bens just before I took chase, but I hoped my billfold was still there in case I needed moula to bribe a fellow cop. So I fished in my suit pocket and found it along with my detective badge. I thought I was ready for whatever came my way— but I wasn't.

"Mr. Collier?" said a disembodied voice.

I nearly jumped out of my seat when I heard the voice because there was no one in the room. "Yeah," I answered. "What's it to you?"

"Tug Collier?" said a second voice.

"What's going on? Why am I being held?"

"You're not being held. You came to us," said the first voice.

"You came to the light," said the second voice.

"So where am I? What do you want from me?"

"Nothing. But, someone is looking for you."

"You mean the coward who tried to shoot me in the back?"

"No. A woman is looking for you," the first voice explained.

"Greta," I asked.

"No. Sarah Williams," the second voice replied.

"Who?"

"Sarah Williams," the voice repeated.

"I don't know nobody by that name."

"She's in Chicago by way of Los Angeles, and she'd like to get to know you."

"What woman wouldn't?" I joked.

"Mother Teresa," said the first voice.

"Who?"

"Never mind," the voice continued. "Sarah Williams seems to have taken an interest in you."

"Why?"

"She thinks she might have a job for you, and she would like to meet you."

"What kind of job?

"She didn't say. You'll have to ask her yourself."

"Well then, how about I meet her?" I smiled.

"We were hoping you'd say that."

The next instant, I fell through the floor of the room and found myself falling again into darkness, but this time, my head started to spin as I fell. The rush of the air around me was ferocious, and it nearly deafened me. Then in an instant, my fall came to a screeching halt. When I opened my eyes, I found myself in an enormous room filled with books. It was night time, and the place was deserted except for a lone woman who was lost in her research. I decided to approach her. The closer I got to her, the more I realized she had the potential to be a looker. She was very well built, but she seemed to be a brainy sort and did her best to keep her looks under wraps. She wore glasses with thick black frames like a machine shop worker. Her thick, curly black hair looked like she just got out of bed which was a look I loved. She didn't wear make-up, but then again she didn't need it.

Before I got closer to her, I slipped into an aisle and pretended to be interested in a book ... which was quite an acting job for me. She never looked up. I pulled another book off the shelf and examined it. Every book was stamped "Property of Chicago". It turned out I was in the Chicago Public Library. As a police detective I drove past the library many times, but I never stopped inside. Somehow I never figured on it being this big. But, something seemed to be very wrong. I walked around behind the woman and stood close enough to her that she had to sense I was there. But, she still didn't look up or notice me once. She sat in front of some kind of silver screen that looked like a miniature movie theatre screen like the one at the Biograph Movie Theatre on Lincoln Avenue. Words and pictures kept popping up on it. She seemed mesmerized by it so I figured maybe that's why she didn't notice me. I decided to take a chance, and I walked up directly behind her so I could see what she was looking at. It was a cover story of The *Chicago Daily Examiner* from March 30, 1931. My picture was on the front page and the headline read: "Police Detective Murdered in Cold Blood". I laughed out loud and said, "That's a lot of hooey!" But she still didn't react to me. This babe was either playing hard to get or she was deaf.

If it was March 30th of 1931, it was just one day later. Somehow that didn't seem possible. I floated for so long, I lost track of time. I checked the wrist watch Greta gave me for my eighteenth birthday, but it had stopped at midnight. Sometimes, when you have a traumatic incident like I did, it's possible to become disoriented. Once I got hit in the head with a blackjack, and I went to dreamland for a month. All that month I felt like I was trapped inside a coffin, and I thought they were going to bury me, so I kept fighting to get out. The cop who was guarding me said, when I came out of the coma, I came out fighting and punched the doctor who was examining me. I guess during the exam the doctor tapped me one time too often with his little rubber mallet and accidentally found my starter button. I apologized to him once I got back to being myself and thanked him for jump-starting me again.

I watched the woman reach into her purse and pull out a little silver box with a bunch of buttons on it. She pushed a button on the box, and it lit up like the other silver screen. A bunch of numbers came up on the screen, and she pecked at the buttons and set the box down. It rang almost like a telephone, and a man's voice came out of it. I guess she wasn't deaf because she answered him, "Erjon, it's Sarah Williams. I found the article about the guy we're looking for. He did exist. His name was Tug Collier. He was a small time Chicago police detective who was dirty. Somebody shot him in the back and killed him nearly eighty years ago."

If I had any blood left in my body, it would have drained out of my face. While she yabba-dabba-dooed into the little box with buttons, I decided to check out the newspaper story. The story said the cops found me dead on the scene. My car was found a block away with an unidentified woman in the front seat who had been shot between the eyes. Suddenly, I felt a hand on my arm. I turned; it was Greta. Her eyes were very sad. She leaned forward to kiss me on the cheek as if to say everything was okay, but just before she did, she faded away and disappeared.

The Great Depressions of Tug Collier
will be available in late 2017.

About the Author

JoBe Cerny is a writer, actor, producer, and director who has worked on over 9,000 artistic projects and won over 350 major awards. His versatile voice has allowed him to voice many famous animated characters and he also spent three years directing the ultimate conflict of good and evil, *The Word of Promise*, an audio Bible nominated for Audio Book of the Year. It features hundreds of famous actors from around the world and is hailed as a masterpiece.

Cerny grew up in Cicero, Illinois, a town known for real-life conflicts of good and evil. Cicero didn't have a teen gang problem because it was the home of organized crime and Al Capone. Over the years, many illegal activities involving drugs, gambling, gun-smuggling, prostitution, theft, murder-for-hire, and political corruption took place in Cicero.

Attendance for Cerny's fortieth high-school reunion was small because many of his classmates were serving fifty to life. His grandfather was a police magistrate who taught him to shoot a shotgun at the age of six. Later in life, Cerny served in the Army and learned to use many different kinds of weapons.

Cicero was always an ethnic melting pot, and Cerny worked his way through college with a pick and shovel for a Cicero sewer company. While the Taylor Street Files are fictional, they accurately depict the real-life sights and activities he observed on the streets of Cicero and Chicago as a life-long resident. As a cast member of Chicago's The Second City, he honed his sense of humor portraying colorful characters he met on the streets.

One last word of warning: Mr. Cerny is always on the lookout for unusual crimes, and his criminals are each one-of-a-kind. He prides himself in writing mysteries that give the reader a fair chance to solve the mystery. If you like great mysteries, complex villains, and black humor, come join the detectives of Taylor Street as they wage war against a new millennium of Chicago crime.

www.ingramcontent.com/pod-product-compliance
Lightning Source LLC
Chambersburg PA
CBHW070303260626
47160CB00003B/694